Alfred Heales

The archaeology of the Christian altar in Western Europe

with its adjuncts, furniture, and ornaments

Alfred Heales

The archaeology of the Christian altar in Western Europe
with its adjuncts, furniture, and ornaments

ISBN/EAN: 9783741189838

Manufactured in Europe, USA, Canada, Australia, Japa

Cover: Foto ©Andreas Hilbeck / pixelio.de

Manufactured and distributed by brebook publishing software
(www.brebook.com)

Alfred Heales

The archaeology of the Christian altar in Western Europe

PREFACE.

IT seems somewhat singular that a subject of such special interest should never have been taken up, but, so far as I am aware, such is the case.

The present Pamphlet was prepared from notes and extracts casually made, as opportunity offered, during many years past, arranged for the purpose of two lectures for the St. Paul's Ecclesiological Society, and now somewhat extended. It is, however, but a sketch of the subject. In consideration of the purpose for which it was prepared, I have avoided controversial points as much as possible, and in the examples referred-to have chosen preferentially neighbouring localities, and also the more readily accessible authorities. Where foreign examples are noted, without reference to any authority, they are cited from my own observations. Those who desire more information on the subject generally will find much information in Dr. Rock's "Hierurgia" and "Church of our Fathers,"

supplemented, as to post-Reformation times, by the
Rev. J. Fuller-Russell's " Hierurgia Anglicana." Sir
Robert Phillimore's grand work on " Ecclesiastical
Law" is essential, and Chancellor Harington's book
on "Consecration of Churches" useful ; the Ecclesiastical Glossaries of the late Canon Mackenzie Walcott
and Dr. F. G. Lee will be needed for reference ;
while the works of the learned Recorder of Salisbury
(J. D. Chambers), the Rev. Charles Walker, and
Mr. James Parker, will be studied by all who wish to
understand the subject, as bearing upon ritual questions at the present day.

LIST OF AUTHORITIES AND WORKS

QUOTED OR DIRECTLY REFERRED TO.

———◆———

ACTS OF PARLIAMENT :—
        59 George III, c. 134.
        2 & 3 William IV, c. 61.
ÆLFRIC ; Paschal Homily.
Anastatic Drawing Society.
Antiquaries, Society of ; Proceedings.
Archæologia Cantiana.
Archæological Journal.
AUGUSTINE (ST.) ; De Civitate Dei.
Ayenbite of Ynwyt.
AYLIFFE ; Canon Law.

BERJEAU ; History of the Cross.
———— Livres Zylographiques.
Bible en Francoiʒ.
BINGHAM ; Christian Antiquities (Ed. 1855).
Book of Common Prayer.
———————— (First), Edward VI.
BOURASSÉ ; Cathédrales de France.
BRAND ; Popular Antiquities.
BURCKARD ; Misse Secundarie.

Camden Society ; Bury Wills.
Canons, Constitutions, & Excerpts :—A.D. 760, 960, 1075, 1229, 1640.
CARDWELL ; Documentary Annals.
CAUMONT ; Abécédaire.
Church Review.
Church Times.

COATES ; History of Reading.
COLLIER ; Ecclesiastical History.
Coronation Service.
CRANMER ; Reformatio Legum.
CUSSANS ; Herts. Church Goods.

DIGBY ; Compitum.
Dublin, Trinity Church Obits.
DUGDALE ; History of St. Paul's.
DURANDUS ; Rationale.
Durham, Rites.

Early English Homilies.
Early English Text Society.
Essex Archæological Society.
Exodus.

FAIRHOLT ; Dictionary of Terms of Art.
Fasciculus Temporum.

Gesta Henrici V.
GIBSON ; Codex.
GREGORY IX ; Decretals.

HARINGTON ; Consecration of Churches.
HAYDN ; Dictionary of Dates.
Hebrews xiii.
Historical Society.
HUME ; History of England.

Irish Archæological Society.

JOHNSON ; Ecclesiastical Laws and Canons.
JOHNSON ; Notes of Cases.

LABARTE ; Handbook of Arts.
LACROIX ; Life in the Middle Ages.
Lambeth Archiepiscopal Registers.
LEE ; Glossary, Liturgical and Ecclesiastical.
Legenda Aurea (1519).

Legenda Sanctorum (1486).
London and Middlesex Archæological Society.
LUBKE; Ecclesiastical Art in Germany.
LYNDWOOD; Provinciale.

MAITLAND; Church in Catacombs.
Manuale Curatorum (1514).
MARRIOTT; Vestiarium Christianum.
Merton Priory Cartulary (Cotton MSS.).
'MILMAN; History of St. Paul's.
MILBOURN; History of St. Mildred, Poultry.
MULLOOLY; Painting at San Clemente.
MYRC; Parish Priest.

NICHOLS; Manners and Customs.
———— Royal Wills.
———— Testamenta Vetusta.
NORTHCOTE; The Catacombs.

PARKER, JAS.; Archæology of Rome.
————J. H.; Glossary of Architecture.
Parker Society Publications.
PEACOCK; Lincolnshire Church Goods.
PHILLIMORE; Ecclesiastical Law.
Pontifical, York.
Pontificale Romanum; ibid., c. 1500.
PRYNNE; Canterbury's Doom.
PUGIN; Rood-screens.
PULLAN; Altar and Baldacchino.

RIDDLE; Manual of Christian Antiquities.
ROBERTSON; Ecclesiastical Reports.
ROCK; Church of our Fathers.
———— Hierurgia.
Roman Missal.
RUSSELL; Hierurgia Anglicana.

Sarum Missal.
SCOBELL; Acts and Ordinances.
SEVILLA, Descripcion del Templo Catedral

Shakespeare ; Henry V.
Simmons ; Lay Folks' Mass Book.
Sparrow ; Articles and Injunctions.
Spelman ; Concilia.
Strutt ; Regal and Ecclesiastical Antiquities.
Surtees Society Publications.

Testamenta Eboracensia.
Tyssen ; Surrey Church Goods.
Walcott ; Glossary of Sacred Archæology.
Waterlow ; Accounts of St. Michael, Cornhill.
Webb ; Continental Ecclesiology.
Wilkins ; Concilia.
Woolnoth ; Canterbury Cathedral.
Wright ; Nominale of Fifteenth Century.

THE ALTAR.

ALTAR AT ST. APOLLINARE NUOVO, RAVENNA, A.D. 570.

THE TERM "ALTAR."

THE term "Altar," as applied to the structure on which the Holy Sacrament is celebrated, has first to be considered. Although the word is that most frequently used in ecclesiastical language (as by St. Paul, "We have an altar"[1]) and in common parlance, yet, whether the material be stone or wood, it is, in fact, synonymous with the terms "Mensa Domini," "God's Board," or "The Holy Table." Ancient writers used both names indifferently; Mede thinks that the word *altar* was usually adopted for the first two

---

Hebrews xiii, 10.

centuries, and that the word table is not to be found in the works of any author of those ages now existing.[1] One or other of these terms is generally adopted in the Prayer Book. Thus, in a cautela to the Sarum Missal:—

> Presbyter in *mensd* Christe, quid agis bene pensa :
> Aut tibi vita datur, aut mors eterna paratur.

And so in the famous sequence, " Lauda Sion," used on Corpus Christi Day, which will be found in the Sarum Missal from whence our own Communion Service is almost translated:[2]—

> In hac *mensd* novi Regis,
> Novum pascha nove legis,
> Phase vetus terminat.

In the first English Prayer Book, issued in 1549 under authority of the proclamation of King Edward VI, the terms *Lord's table* and *God's board* are also used, though more frequently the word *altar*,[3] and *that* at a time when stone was the only material used. The same practice has prevailed ever since, as in the Canons of 1640, wherein it is declared that " it may be called an altar in that sense in which the primitive church called it an altar." In the Coronation Service[4] it is always called the altar; the term is also used in some Church Building Acts. And in the narrative of aristocratic weddings, such as daily appear in the newspapers, it is always specified that the bride was led to the " altar:" no doubt it may be said that the reference here is to the hymeneal altar; but one can scarcely in fairness assume a reference to a pagan and idolatrous rite in the description of a solemn Christian ceremony.

Christ's board is another term by which it was and is known in English vernacular. A few examples of this use (commencing at a time when stone was becoming the almost invariable material of the structure) may be given. Ælfric,

---

[1] Bingham; Christian Antiquities, Bk. VIII, c. vi, s. 12. (Oxf. Ed., 1855, III, p. 90.)

[2] Sarum Missal; Festival of Corpus Christi.

[3] Parker Society's reprint.

[4] Reprinted in Phillimore's Ecclesiastical Law, p. 1074.

in his celebrated Paschal Homily, written in the twelfth century, speaks of Christ's board :[1]—

> þat holie bord bugen ʒ þat bred bruken. (Go to the holy board and partake of the bread.)

And further on :—

> þanne muge we bicumeliche to *godes bord* bugen, ʒ his bode wurðliche bruken. (Then may we go meekly to God's board, and worthily partake of his body.)[2]

The Ayenbite of Ynwyt, written early in the fourteenth century, says :—

> Yet eft hi ssolle by more clene / and more holy / nor þet hi serueð at *godes borde* of his coupe / of his breade / and of his wyne / and of his mete. Godes table is þe wyeued. þe coupe is þe chalis, his bread and his wyn ; þet is his propre bodi and his propre blod.[3]

Lydgate, in his Vertue of the Masse, speaks of the

Altar called *God's board*.[4]

And Robert of Brunne, in the same century :—

> Richard at *Godes bord* His messe had ʒ his rights.[5]

By these instances, it will be seen clearly that the terms "Altar," "Table of the Lord," "Holy Table," and "God's Board," have been used synonymously from very early times.

FORM, STRUCTURE, AND MATERIAL.

From the name we will proceed to the structure and material.

The oldest existing Christian altar is preserved in the Basilica of St. John Lateran, at Rome, and is believed, by tradition which has come down from a very early period, to

---

[1] Early English Text Society ; Early English Homilies, II, p. 95.
[2] Parker Society's reprint, p. 99.
[3] Ayenbite of Ynwyt ; Early English Text Society, pp. 235, 236.
[4] Ibid., p. 233.
[5] Langtoft's Chronicle. Hearne, p. 182 ; quoted in the preceding.

have been used by St. Peter; and so highly was the altar
esteemed that, between the years 1362 and 1370, a stone
baldacchino was erected over it, wherein are enshrined the
heads, as it is believed, of SS. Peter and Paul. The altar has
the special dignity of being the only wooden altar allowed by
the Roman Church;[1] it alone contains no relics;[2] and no one
but the pope himself officiates at it. It presents, therefore, a
typical example of the earliest description of Christian altar.
It consists of a mensa or table, nearly square, and formed
of a broad, rather thick wooden plank, resting on four legs,
which, with the intervening spaces, are covered in by three
planks on each face; the table extends considerably beyond
the frame of legs, and the whole height is about four feet;
it is said to be of cypress wood, and the surface has the
appearance of having been planed.[3]

Wood continued to be the material generally used during
the first four or five centuries.[4] Wooden altars are mentioned
by Optatus, and by SS. Athanasius and Augustine of Hippo,
and the material was deemed a reminiscence of the cross of
Calvary.[5] In 509, the Council of Epone, in France, practically required that stone should be the material used, by
decreeing that no altar should be consecrated with the chrism
of holy oil but such as were of stone.[6] But in England
wooden altars continued in more or less use till the end of
the eleventh century, when stone was ordered as being a
more suitable material. A canon made under Archbishop
Lanfranc, in 1075, directed the change;[7] and, according to
William of Malmesbury, stone altars were introduced into

---

[1] Durandus; Rationale, I, vii (Neale & Webb's Translation, p. 28).
[2] Lubke; Ecclesiastical Art in Germany, English Ed., p. 115.
[3] Webb; Continental Ecclesiology, p. 508; a most valuable collection
of church notes, by the eminent ecclesiologist, the Rev. Benjamin Webb,
one of our vice-presidents.
[4] Rock; Hierurgia, p. 493.
[5] Vide Sacred Archæology, by the Rev. Mackenzie Walcott, *s. v.* "Altar,"
for this and some other statements. He does not state the sources of his
information : but, in this case, probably Bingham ; Christian Antiquities,
Bk. VIII, c. vi, s. 15.
[6] Glossary of Architecture, *s. v.* "*Altar*," &c.
[7] Johnson ; Collection of Ecclesiastical Laws, Canons, &c.

England by St. Wulstan of Worcester, who died in 1095. In Ireland, a canon of Archbishop Comyn, in 1186, prohibited any celebration on a wooden table according to the then usage, but permitted the introduction of a small piece of stone into the middle of the wooden mensa.[1] Probably the like provision was adopted in the examples of wooden altars which we occasionally find mentioned at all dates; as, for example, in 1432, in the will of Sir John Raventhorp, priest of the Chapel of St. Martin, Aldwerk:—

Item lego aliud vestimentum cum *altari ligneo* predictæ capellæ.[2]

And so in the case of a wooden altar, mentioned by Erasmus as existing in Canterbury Cathedral. Wooden frames are represented in the famous stained glass at Long Melford, Suffolk, dating near the end of the fifteenth century,[3] and not uncommonly in illuminations. In the unchanging Eastern Church, and in the Russian branch, wood continues to be used. Stone altars are supposed by some to have been derived from the use in the catacombs, where the bodies of the eminent deceased were deposited in niches scooped out near the ground level, and a conch-shaped hollow above, leaving a flat table of rock between, upon which the divine mysteries were celebrated. At all events, stone became the favourite material at an early date; for we find that (as already mentioned), in the year 509, a canon of the Council of Epone directed that no altar should be consecrated with chrism unless constructed of stone.

The top was originally a nearly square slab resting on supports in every variety. In the remarkable examples existing at Ravenna, and in others represented in the mosaics there, altars appear either as tables[4] or as solid

---

[1] Book of Obits of Trinity Church, Dublin, published by the Irish Archæological Society; note to preface, p. xxi.

[2] Testamenta Eboracensia; Surtees Society, II, p. 29.

[3] London and Middlesex Archæological Society's Transactions; Evening Meetings, 1871, p. 18.

[4] See illustration at p. 28, *post*, from mosaic at San Vitale, Ravenna, which was consecrated by St. Maximinianus, A.D. 547.

cubes.[1] Every variety of form may be found, and though
probably the table was the most usual type at an early
date, the contour of one of the Ravenna examples,
probably dating in the eighth century, resembles a chest of
drawers, reminding one of the Royal Library at Berlin,
which is said to have been designed on the upholstery model.
It is recorded that when Pope Vigilius (in the sixth century)
fled from the soldiers of Justinian to St. Peter's Church,
he there clung to the legs of the altar of St. Euphemius,
till the faithful flocked round and drove away the soldiers
and rescued him.   And although from the thirteenth century
the solid, tomb-like form generally prevailed in the Western
Church (to which my remarks chiefly relate), and superseded
the tabular form, yet every variety of the latter may be found
even to the present date.   Most usually attached to the wall
by the back edge of the slab, the weight was sometimes
supported on a single short pillar; more often there were
three pillars or legs, and still more frequently five, the largest
of which was in the centre and the others near the angles.
Sometimes the table rested on slabs set up edgewise at each
extremity, or in minor instances on merely a bracket attached
to the wall.

PAROCHIAL ALTAR OF ARUNDEL CHURCH, SUSSEX.

The most usual type, however, from the thirteenth century,
was that of a solid-looking parallelogram, sometimes formed
of a single block of stone, as in the cathedrals of Speyer

---

[1] The illustration at the head of this monograph is made from a sketch,
by the writer, of an altar in the Church of St. Apollinare Nuovo, Ravenna,
which church was built by Theodoric, in the sixth century, as the cathedral for his Arian bishops; subsequently consecrated to the use of the
orthodox, and receiving its present dedication in the ninth century.

(Spires) and Como, and at Vienne in France. Occasionally
the block was hollowed out in order to contain relics. It will
be remembered how Harold, after ratifying by an oath his
renunciation of the crown of England, found with dismay that
relics had been concealed in the altar on which, in order to
give the act a greater solemnity, he had placed his hand.[1]
Examples of altars thus hollowed are not very frequently to
be met with now, but there is one in Regensburg (Ratisbon)
Old Dom, where the altar is formed of one great block of
stone 6 feet by nearly 5 feet, and 3 feet 6 inches high, but
excavated in such manner as to leave no doubt of the fact
that it was intended to contain relics. Minor altars were
occasionally hollowed for use as Easter sepulchres,[2] but I do
not happen to have seen or heard of any ancient existing
example. They sometimes even served as an aumbry, or
cupboard, for books and vestments, of which a curious example
may be noted where Richard Russell, by his Will, in the year
1435, leaves a bequest for making an altar in his parish church
of St. John, Hungate, York ;

> Quod unum altare fiat bene et effectualiter de tabulis in parte
> boriali dictæ ecclesiæ coram ymaginibus Beatæ Mariæ et Sanctæ
> Annæ, et subtus idem altare, unum almariolum pro libris et
> vestimentis idem altari pertinentibus, fideliter conservandis.[3]

Such an arrangement was condemned by a Provincial Council
held at Toulouse in 1590.[4]

In accordance with the usage of Christianity to assimilate
to itself things which had been intended for other religions
(thus converting them from the service of false gods to that
of the one true God)—and other things which had previously
had no religious association—ancient sarcophagi and baths
were converted into Christian altars, for which, indeed, they
were eminently fitted in form (though the sculpture was often

---

[1] Hume; History of England, c. iii (Hughes' Ed., I, p. 137).
[2] Vide Wilkins; Concilia, I, p. 497.
[3] Beneath the altar an aumbry, or cupboard, in which to preserve the
books and vestments of the altar. Testamenta Eboracensia, II, p. 53;
Surtees Society.
[4] Notes by Canon Simmons to Lay Folks' Mass Book; Early English
Text Society.

singularly unsuitable); and the excavated interior was ready
for the reception of relics, which, as will be mentioned later,
were usually considered necessary to the due consecration of
the altar. Thus it happens that at Rome, where such objects
would naturally be most frequently obtained, there are ancient
examples of baths and sarcophagi, formed of granite, basalt,
porphyry, alabaster, and marble, since pressed into the Christian service as altars.[1]

Altars are of all sizes: the *mensa*, or *table*, as it is techni-
cally termed—*i. e.*, the top—varying from 3 feet to 13 feet,
or more, in length. The high altar at St. Peter's, Rome, is
25 feet square.[2] The Arundel altar measures 12 feet 6 inches
long, and one at Immensee, which I measured, is about 16 by 7
feet, but I do not think this example is of great antiquity, for
it is unmarked by the five small crosses which, it must be
observed, were anciently invariably incised in the upper
surface—viz., one in the centre, and one near each angle—
generally plain, though I have seen them *pomée*, and, rarely,
set saltierwise. In the still subsisting altar in the Chapel of
Broughton Castle there are incised nine crosses. At the time
when stone altars were destroyed in this country, the mensa,
or table, was frequently set in the pavement of the church,
especially near a doorway, in order that it might so be most
readily and effectually desecrated and worn; pious care, unable
to prevent further wrong, sometimes laid it in the chancel
floor, or beneath the spot occupied by the "decent frame"
by which it was superseded;[3] and occasionally the upper
surface was turned downwards in the pavement, and so preserved from destruction or further desecration. Not unfrequently these stones may be still found in the pavement of
our chancels, when they may at once be identified by the five
small crosses engraved upon them, viz., one in the centre,

---

[1] Parker; Archæology of Rome, XI, p. 85. Abundant examples will
be seen by travellers in Italy and the South of France.
[2] Bingham; Christian Antiquities, Ed. 1855, III. p. 98.
[3] England does not stand alone in this form of desecration, though
foreign examples are rare; there is an altar-slab in the pavement of the
north aisle of the noble Church of Limburg, on the Larne, and others
may here and there be noted.

and one near each corner; some of them have been restored
to their proper use.

In very rare cases, of which there is an instance in the
baptistery at Ratisbon, the mensa is composed of more than one
piece; though this is contrary to ecclesiastical order, for Pope
Innocent directed that the altar should be of one stone, for
its construction of several pieces would be a symbol of the
church divided by error and schisms.[1]

ALTAR OF THE CHURCH OF ST. GERMER.

Occasionally the front of the altar was enriched with
carved arcading and sculpture,[2] but after the thirteenth century the very general rule north of Italy was to leave it a
perfectly plain surface of walling, covered by a moveable
frontal of any precious material from gold downwards, and in
this country usually of embroidery; but a notice of such
frontals must be reserved until we treat upon the adjuncts to
the altar.

In speaking ecclesiologically of the front of an altar the
terms *middle,* and *right* and *left* sides were used, and these

[1] Rock; Church of our Fathers, I, p. 246.
[2] Among the abundant examples engraved, it will suffice to refer to
Labarte's Handbook of the Arts of the Middle Ages, English Edition,
pp. 241 and 242; and a magnificent specimen in Lacroix' Military and
Religious Life in the Middle Ages, English Edition, p. 219. The illustration given above is taken from Caumont's Abécédaire; Architecture
Religieuse, p. 241.

latter terms were never applied by canonists or ecclesiastical writers to the north and south ends. The rubrical directions always specified the position of the priest as *in medium altare*, or *dextra* or *sinistra parte* or *cornu altaris*. And here we may note that the Sarum Missal, in speaking of the right or left of the altar, refers to the right or left of the officiating priest; while in the Roman rite, since 1458, the reverse is the case, the right and left referring to the right or left of the crucifix upon the altar, which necessarily faces the priest. In the south of Europe—as, for example, Spain—they always speak of the Epistle and Gospel sides *(el lado de la Epistola* and *el lado del Evangelio)* with the same meaning. I am informed that, in the authentic Welsh version of our Prayer Book, the word there used for north "side" cannot possibly be applied to the north "end,"[1] a fact which confirms the opinion of every canonist that the term used in our English version did not mean "end." [2]

NUMBER AND POSITION.

Originally, as typifying the unity of Christ and His Church, there was but one altar in each church, as referred to by SS. Ignatius, Irenæus, and Cyprian, and by Tertullian and Eusebius of Cæsarea; and such is still the case in the East, though they have other altars in detached oratories around the building. It was this ancient usage to which the English Church reverted for its general rule, though there is no canon to prevent more than one altar in a church where more are required as a matter of convenience. At an early date the number was increased; thus, we read that Constantine the Great had three in the Church of the Holy Sepulchre in

---

[1] I am indebted for this information to Mr. H. W. King, Hon. Sec. to the Essex Archæological Society, a learned ecclesiologist as well as archæologist.

[2] Canon Simmons, whose predilections I assume to be definitely non-ritualistic, says : "So far as I have observed, *end* never was so used (i.e., to mean the narrower side) by any early writer when speaking of an English altar, but invariably as of the north or south part of the western side. (Lay Folks' Mass Book; Early English Text Society, p. 179.)

Jerusalem, and four in the Church of St. Mary in the Valley of Jehoshaphat. In the year 326, Bishop Aventius consecrated three at Avignon, and in the same century we hear of seven in the Lateran Church at Rome. In the sixth century, Pope Leo the Great mentions thirteen erected by Palladius, Bishop of Saintes, in honour of the apostles. St. Gregory of Tours refers to two in the Church of St. Peter, Bordeaux, and that he had celebrated upon three in the Church of Brennes; while the building plan of the Church of St. Gall, in the ninth century, indicates the spots allotted to no less than seventeen. There were in St. Paul's Cathedral, at the time of the surrender, thirty-five chantries, each having an endowment for from one to three priests;[1] and their value was so important as to cause a special Act of Confiscation, by which they were all escheated to the Crown, that is, to no national purpose, but for the benefit of the greedy brigands of courtiers who were then in the ascendant.[2] At Durham there were thirty-six altars, each with a double set of requisites, viz., frontals, chalices, censers, ships, and candlesticks.[3] At Canterbury Cathedral there were about twenty-four.[4] In some cathedrals, and even parish churches, their number became multiplied to what must be deemed a very unnecessary extent, as in the churches of St. Mary, Dantzig, and St. Elizabeth, Breslau, each of which contains about fifty altars.[5] The arrangement at Ypres may be commended for simplicity and moderation; the high altar stands behind the easternmost pair of pillars in the choir, and another is in the apse behind; at the end of each aisle is one, and one more in the north chapel completes the whole number. As an example of an ordinary English church we may refer to St. Michael, Cornhill, which had six.[6]

1549. Pd. to ye mason in Gracyous strete for takyng downe vj aulters, xvj^s. x^d.

---

[1] Dugdale ; History of St. Paul's Cathedral, p. 380, et seq.
[2] Dean Milman ; History of St. Paul's, pp. 145—150.
[3] Rites of Durham ; Surtees Society, p. 82.
[4] Woolnoth ; Canterbury Cathedral, p. 113.
[5] Walcott, and others.
[6] St. Michael, Cornhill, Churchwardens' Accounts (privately printed by Mr. Alfred J. Waterlow), p. 75.

At an early date, when the basilica became (or became the type for) the fabric of the church, the altar was always located in the chord of the apse; behind it stood the celebrant facing it and the people, while round the apse were the seats for the bishop and clergy and assistants, whence was drawn the symbolism of the bishop at the helm steering the barque of the Church. This arrangement, so far as relative positions of the altar and the seats for the bishop, clergy, and choir ranged round and behind it, occurs very frequently in Italy and the south of France and Germany; and even the position of the celebrant facing the people is still in occasional use in certain churches, chiefly in Rome, which are termed basilicas and possess special privileges. The rubric of the Ambrosian rite assumes such to be the ordinary arrangement, and therefore at the benediction and " Pax vobiscum," the celebrant is not directed to turn to the people, as he is already facing towards them; and the same use is admitted in the Roman Church.[1] But it must be borne in mind that where the basilican arrangement was practised, and the officiating priest stood behind the altar and facing the people, the apse was at the west end of the building, so that he faced eastward while officiating; when the church was subsequently extended eastwards by the erection of a chancel or choir the altar was always placed there, and the priest, still facing east, necessarily had his back to the people.

The idea of reverting to the basilican arrangement, so far as regards the position of the celebrant, appears to have occurred to some of the Reformers; for we find that at Canterbury, in Archbishop Parker's time, at all events when there was no celebration of the Holy Communion, the priest stood on the east side of the altar; and Bishop Jewel refers to the custom as in use in various Italian and other churches: while a singular instance of an arrangement made in the time of the Puritans exists to the present day at Deerhurst,

---

[1] Advertendum est quod si altare est versus populum, et in eo celebrans stat facie populo verso, non se vertit aliter cum dicturus est "Dominus tecum," &c. Ordo pro Misse Secundarie. By John Burckard, Prothonotary of the Holy See; revised. Rome, 1508.

Gloucestershire, where there are seats all round the chancel; and the like at Langley Chapel, Shropshire; but in these cases the holy table was placed endwise.

It was either the change of position of the celebrant which thus led to the removal of altars from the west to the east end of the churches, or else such removal of altars which led first to the change of position of the celebrant and, next, to the building of chancels. Wherever there is a chancel it forms the east end of the church; such at least was invariably the case in all northern Europe, though in Rome and Italy they seem to have had as little regard for orientation as any non-conformists have here at the present day.

At Maintz on the Rhine, at Verdun in France, and some other cathedrals, there is an altar at each end of the building, that at the east being the high altar, daily used, while that at the opposite end is only used on special occasions, and then the celebrant occupies the basilican position;[1] and this was the case at Canterbury Cathedral, in the late Anglo-Saxon period, where, in an oratory at the far west end of the nave, the priest stood with his face to the people.[2] The cathedrals of Freiburg (in Breisgau) and Constance have an altar at each end of the choir. In some cathedrals, as at Padua, Bologna, and Assisi, the high altar is so arranged as to be used by the priest standing either facing or back to the people. At Spoleto the altar is of double width, divided lengthwise by a low reredos on which stand the candles; the altar-cross faces east, towards the choir-stalls which are ranged round the apse.

The high altar is defined by our great canonist, Lyndwood, to be that of him to whom the church is dedicated,[3] and therefore placed in the choir or most solemn part. In the case of cathedrals and monastic churches of very great size, it usually stands in the chord of the apse, but sometimes it is brought forward one or more bays (as now at St. Paul's), or even

---

[1] Webb; Continental Ecclesiology. Bourassé; Cathédrales de France, p. 477.
[2] Rock; Church of our Fathers, I, p. 226.
[3] Lyndwood; Provinciale, seu constitutiones Angliæ: Oxford Ed., fol. 1679, p. 252.

under the central tower or dome: Trent, Angoulême, Spires, and Madrid will serve as examples. In parish churches, where the choir is apsidal, which is very generally the case on the continent, the high altar was placed in the chord; but in England, where square east ends are almost invariable, it was set against the east wall, though sometimes, but very rarely, detached from it. But wherever it was, its position was permanent, and most unquestionably it was not subject to be moved from time to time as a matter of convenience; and (though it was solely for the reason that stone altars are not of a readily locomotive nature that a former Judge of the Arches Court of Canterbury declared them to be illegal) the same idea has still maintained itself, for we find a Church Building Act in the reign of King George III,[1] directing that where a church was built upon a site part of which was in one jurisdiction and part in another, the whole should be subject to the jurisdiction within which the altar was locally situated; thus the effect of moving the altar might, in such a case, operate as a transfer of ecclesiastical jurisdiction. This Act and this provision are referred to in a subsequent Act, which was passed in the reign of His late Majesty, King William IV.[2]

When other altars became multiplied they were placed in all parts of the church. Behind the choir of a cathedral was a lady chapel, flanked by a range of smaller chapels usually radiating from the choir-aisle, or ambulatory, which was generally carried round the apse of the choir; and in these the altars were always placed on the east side, or as nearly east as the form of the chapel would allow, and it is only in more modern times that the altars have been placed as we generally see them in foreign cathedrals, at the far end of the chapels without regard to their orientation. The choir being usually bounded on the west by a rood-screen, an altar was, in the case of a monastic church, placed on the outer side of the screen for the use of the parishioners; it was ordinarily dedicated to the Holy Cross, and at Worcester Cathedral was

---

[1] Act of Parliament, 59 Geo. III, c. 134, s. 7.
[2] Act of Parliament, 2 & 3 William IV, c. 61.

called the middle or Mattin altar. At St. Alban's there are evident marks about the screen of an altar having been there.[1] At Ulm and Meissen Cathedrals are similar examples, the former having for a reredos a carved wood triptych, and the latter an early painting. At Udine, where the practical choir is partly in front of and partly behind the altar, the latter is backed by a screen running across, and the bishop's throne and part of the clergy stalls are behind it. In Durham Cathedral, between the pillars supporting the west side of the lanthorn, over against the choir door, was the *Jesus altar,* where Jesus Mass was sung every Friday throughout the year; behind it was a fair, high, stone wall, with a door on either side for the procession.[2] It would appear that sometimes there was an altar even up in the rood-loft itself, as at St. Maurice, Vienne.[3] Besides these altars, there were very constantly, even in the smallest churches, others at the east end of the aisles; while cathedrals and larger churches had chapels, each with its altar, along the east walls of their transepts, and many others built out between the deep buttresses, either as part of the original plan (as, commonly, in France), or severally erected subsequently (as more usual in this country), and were generally the private chapels of families or confraternities, by whom they were erected and endowed or maintained. We must not omit to note the Chapel of the Nine Altars at Durham Cathedral, where they all stood in a row against the east wall, but probably separated by screens or parcloses. Also, altars were often placed backing against the nave pillars, as, for example, at St. Stephen, Vienna, and Buda; or, in little family monumental chapels, constructed (especially in England) under the arches between the choir or the nave and their respective aisles. At Boppard, on the Rhine, is the singular arrangement of an altar at the east end of each triforium gallery,[4] and the same was the case at Hexham, as appears from the account given by Prior

---

[1] Pugin ; Treatise on Rood-screens, p. 10.
[2] Rites of Durham ; Surtees Society, p. 28.
[3] Pugin ; Rood-screens, p. 17.
[4] Webb ; Continental Ecclesiology. Walcott's Glossary, &c.

Richard, in 1180, of the great church built there by St. Wilfrid;
in fact, Dr. Rock says that this situation was occasionally
adopted from Anglo-Saxon times downwards, and he gives an
example at Gloucester Cathedral;[1] while at Compton, in Surrey,
the eastern half of the chancel was vaulted so as to form a
gallery at half its height, and fitted with the high altar below
and another just over it, both visible to the congregation.

Wherever there was an altar, there was, except in Italy, a
piscina close at hand, and thus when, as so usually happens in
our visit to some old church, we find a piscina we may be quite
certain that there was formerly an altar immediately adjoining.[2]

An arrangement very commonly found in Italy and the
south of France, and the Rhine and in Germany, is that of
raising the choir upon a crypt, while flights of steps lead up to
one and down to the other. In this arrangement, the choir is
raised above the level of the body of the church about as
much as the crypt is below that level. In the crypt, which is
called "The Confessionary," are the relics of the patron saint
placed in a kind of tomb immediately under the high altar,
while against or near the east wall of the crypt, is another
altar. While thus referring to the occasional great elevation
of the choir with this particular object, it may be well to note
that in our English parish churches the chancel and altar
were invariably (unless in consequence of a peculiarity of site,
or some other special reason) very little raised above the level
of the rest of the church, a fact which is shown conclusively
by comparing the relative levels of the piscina and sedilia in
the chancel, and the doorways in the nave and aisles.
Among foreign examples may be noted the noble Cathedral of
Tournay, where the choir is raised but one step above the
level of the nave, the sacrarium one higher, and the altar
four more low steps; and Ypres is similar, except that the
altar is only raised three steps. These facts form an

---

[1] Rock; Church of our Fathers, I, p. 299, note, and p. 231, note.
[2] The piscina is a small niche on the south side of an altar, breast high
from the ground, in the cill of which was a drain to carry away the
rinsings of the chalice; and very generally there is a narrow shelf or
ledge half way up, which served as a credence.

illustration of the mediæval *motif* which designed to deepen
the physical perception of mystery conveyed to worshippers, by
surrounding the chancel with high screens, and guarding the
altar itself with side curtains; contrasting with the modern,
ultramontane practice of throwing down all screens, raising
the altar to a high level, and by all means endeavouring to
lay bare the actual manual acts of celebration to the gaze of
spectators, as though sight were the first essential to faith in
the holy mysteries.

CONSECRATION.

The earliest recorded instance of the consecration of an
altar was that performed by Pope Felix I, c. A.D. 279.[1] The
custom is referred to by St. Gregory Nyssen who was born
in the year 330, and by St. Ambrose; the canon of the
Council of Epone in 509, and the Excerptions of Ecgbriht, in
740, forbade the consecration of altars by unction with chrism
unless they were of stone, and the latter further ordered that
no priest should celebrate except on a hallowed altar.[2] Very
similar enactments were made by the Convocation c. 960,
temp. King Edgar Theodulphus.

An altar may be consecrated by an act independent
of the consecration of the church, in which case it is performed with very similar ceremonies, including chrism, in
remembrance of the anointing of Jacob's pillar.[3] The rubric
states that, although it may be done on any day in the week,
Sunday is the more fit day. Among the requirements are a
vessel containing relics, and three grains of incense, and a
scroll of parchment with an inscription in large letters as to
the relics, the name of the saint in whose honour the altar is
dedicated, and the name of the consecrator, and a note of any
indulgences granted; and by the Constitutions of Henry de
Blois (Bishop of Winchester), in 1229, it was ordered that at
the dedication of a church there should be clearly inscribed,

---

[1] By St. Sylvester, according to Haydn; Dictionary of Dates.
[2] Spelman; Concilia, p. 263. Johnson; Canons.
[3] Pope Innocent III; Decretals of Gregory IX, De Celebratione Mis-
sarum.

circa majus altare, the year and day of dedication, the name
of the dedicator, and the name of the saint in whose honour it
is dedicated;[1] which vessel is carefully sealed by the bishop
officiating, and deposited in a hollow in the altar left for the
purpose, and which hollow is immediately after the com-
pletion of the consecration cemented up by a mason. In the
ceremony, which we must not stay to describe at length,
chrism, oil of catechumens, incense, water, ashes, salt, and
wine are required.[2] The bishop in his seat on the left of the
new altar begins (followed by the others), in a low voice, the
penitential psalms, without litany; he then vests, and taking
his pastoral staff in his left hand, deposits his mitre on the
altar, and proceeds with very much the same ceremony as at
the dedication of a church.[3] Relics are thus required to be
enclosed in the altar as a matter of necessity, according to
Ayliffe, but Lyndwood considers them not to be of the substance of the consecration; and so the York Pontifical says:
" Si debeat recludi reliquiæ, fiat," &c.;[4] and referring to a
practice sometimes used, when, in the absence of relics, the
Holy Sacrament itself was placed in the altar, Lyndwood
objects to such practice, for that the Holy Sacrament ought
not to be kept except for the sick.[5] The consecration of one
altar does not operate to consecrate the other altars in the
same church.[6] Mention of the consecration or hallowing of
altars frequently occurs in parish accounts: thus, at St. Mary-
at-Hill :[7]—

> 1493. Paid to the suffragan of London for halowyng
> St. Stephen's aulter ...   .   x⁸. iiij⁴.

In 1554, the suffragan's fee for hallowing the altar, and a
dinner afterwards cost £1:6s. 11d.

---

[1] Harington; Consecration of Churches, p. 140.
[2] York Pontifical; Surtees Society, p. 104, where the ceremony is given
at full length.
[3] Pontificale ad Usum Romanum; 15 cent.: also York Pontifical; Surtees
Society, p. 137, where the music also is given.
[4] York Pontifical, p. 121.
[5] Ayliffe; Canon Law, p. 195, note. Lyndwood; Provinciale, p. 249.
[6] Decretals of Pope Gregory IX.
[7] St. Mary-at-Hill; Nichols; Illustrations, &c., pp. 101 and 110.

PORTABLE ALTARS.

Portable altars must be briefly adverted to. They were called *altare viaticum, portatile, gestatorium, lapis portatilis, altaria itineraria,* and *super-altars,* indicating their object for use on journeys, in camp, and on visitation of the sick. It is related as an early example that when Charlemagne made his crusade against the pagan Saxons, St. Denis, who accompanied him, had a portable altar. Martene saw three at Paderborn, of which one was believed to have been consecrated by Pope Gregory the Great, and given to St. Augustine for his mission to England. Theodulph's *Capitula,* A.D. 994, apparently refer to portable altars for use with the army.[1] Cranmer's Reformatio Legum, presumably with portable altars in view, proposed to forbid celebration in private houses.[2] A portable altar generally consisted of a small square slab of precious material, such as agate, onyx, jasper on account of its red colour, porphyry or red marble, jet on account of its polish, amethyst, or other valuable stone, set in a frame of gold or silver, enriched with precious stones and enamels; and between the back of the slab and the setting was some relic; the frame often shut up like the wings of a diptych or triptych. Various examples of very early date still exist: a silver one of the Saxon period was found in a coffin (supposed to have been that of St. Cuthbert) at Durham; one of the tenth century, cased with silver, is preserved in the treasury at Oviedo Cathedral; and a magnificent specimen at Munich, in the chapel of the King of Bavaria, dates from the twelfth century and is enriched with precious stones set *en cabochon;*[3] at Salisbury Cathedral there was, in 1222, one set in gold, and at St. George's, Windsor, in 1385, was one of jasper silver bound and gilt, one of alabaster, and four of marble.[4]

---

[1] Johnson; Canons.
[2] Cranmer; Reformatio Legum, p. 91.
[3] See Labarte; Art in the Middle Ages, pp. 222 and 381. Lubke, p. 135. Rock; Church of our Fathers, I, p. 250.
[4] Rock; Church of our Fathers, I, p. 252.

Portable altars were, however, only permitted under very special circumstances, and for very special reasons. An example of a licence to possess one occurs in the additional manuscripts at the British Museum. Pope Innocent IV, in his ninth year (1251), issued a rescript to the Archbishop of York, ordering by his papal authority, and granting to his beloved daughter in Christ, the Countess of Lincoln (who of her devotion, *ferat munera grata*), quod altare posset habere portatile, in quo faceret, sibi et suæ familiæ, Divina officia celebrari.[1] In the middle of the fifteenth century, Pope Nicholas V, of his grace, granted to Archbishop Kempe (of York) permission to concede to ten persons (*decem personis nobilibus*) leave to have a portable altar; the grant was dated at St. Peter's, Rome, the 6th ide of June, 1447, and in the first year of his pontificate. Pursuant to this grant, the archbishop made the concession to nine persons, including a monk of the cathedral church, the master of the college of St. Gregory and Martin of Wy, his own chaplain, one in his service, and the treasurer of his household, and the rest to private individuals.[2]

But (assuming that the term *super altare* meant a *portable altar*, which apparently was the case) they became very common at a later period: here are examples. Katherine, Lady Hastings, by her will in 1503 bequeathed, with two vestments and two mass-books, two super-altars, one of white, to her son Richard, and one of jet to her son William.[3] In 1534, the guild of B. V. Mary of Boston, had five super-altars, whereof four were described as closed in wood, and one of them being larger than the others, and the fifth was without wood.[4] At the dissolution of the famous Abbey of Westminster, in the 30th year of King Henry VIII (1538), they had there[5]—

> Oon superaltare garnysshed with sylver plate and perles and conterfett stonys.

---

[1] Add. MS. 15,357, No. 17. (Vide App. to Archbishop Gray's Register. Printed by the Surtees Society.)
[2] York Pontifical; Surtees Society, p. 386.
[3] Testamenta Vetusta, p. 454.
[4] Peacock; Lincolnshire Church Furniture, p. 205.
[5] Inventory of Goods of Westminster Abbey; London and Middlesex Archæological Transactions, IV, p. 347.

Oon other superaltare garnysshed with plate of sylver, pounsed.

Oon other great superaltare sett in paynted tymber and open in bothe the sydes of the same tymber, the stone therof of the collour of blak jasper.

DESECRATION.

An altar is canonically held to be desecrated by the removal of the mensa, or its grave fracture, or by a change of form of the altar; and a desecration of the high altar had the effect of desecrating the church, so that both needed a reconsecration, though in some cases, as where the fracture was slight, the minor right of reconciliation would suffice.[1]

In a modern case decided by Dr. Lushington, he said: "If the altar (of the church) has been taken down, there must be a reconsecration."[2]

DESTRUCTION.

The general destruction of stone altars which took place in this country in the sixteenth century was viewed by many persons with disfavour, and (amongst others) Day, Bishop of Chichester, refused to take part in it.[3] The destruction seems to have been effected chiefly in pursuance of the lead given by Bishop Ridley in his Injunctions (for no other positive authority appears to be extant), and these Injunctions are believed, for reasons given by Cardwell (whose learning and impartiality in such matters there can be no reason to doubt), to have been issued solely upon his episcopal authority;[4] and from Injunctions of Queen Elizabeth we learn that those of Bishop Ridley had not been universally followed. The Queen's Injunctions, which are rather restrictive of change, recite that in some places the altars were not removed, and add that

---

[1] Excerptions of Ecgbriht, A.D. 740 (Johnson; Canons). Closer examination has shown that, however early they may be, they are not actually so early as this (Canon Simmons, referring to Haddan and Stubbs; Councils, III, p. 403). A like order was made by Pope Innocent III: vide Decretals of Pope Gregory IX, Lib. III.

[2] Notes of Cases, I, p. 368. In the Consistory Court of London.

[3] Walcott; Sacred Archæology.

[4] Cardwell; Documentary Annals, I, p. 82, note.

"saving for uniformity it seems a matter of no moment."[1] The recent trial, upon which it was decided that the chancel and, consequently, the high altar of the once Collegiate Church of Arundel is simply private property (the present owner of which happens to be a Roman Catholic), caused a reference to the well-known fact that the parochial high altar of that church always stood and still stands in the south transept. There is a curious note of it in 1570, when a presentment was made that "in the Church of Arundel certain altars do stand yet still, to the offence of the godly which murmur and speak much against the same, and the preachers have also spoken against the standing thereof in their sermons of late."[2] Our engraving (p. 6, *ante*) shows it as it is, unaltered.

The proceeds of the sale of the materials of the altars destroyed at the period of the Reformation were in the first place expended in making good the site and wall damaged by the removal, though they did not always suffice,—as for example at St. Mary Colechurch, London, where the altar was sold for 11s. 8d., while the parish spent upon the taking down, levelling the ground, and paving, 58s. 4d.;[3] and any surplus that there might be was generally spent in repairs of the fabric of the church, but sometimes applied to other uses without pretence of decency, as at Rayleigh, Essex, where the parish, out of the proceeds of the sale of sacred vessels, organs, and other church goods, paid 20s. to the stage players that played there on Trinity Sunday.[4]

The base uses to which the consecrated slab was sometimes applied, appears from the statements recorded by King Edward the Sixth's Commissioners; thus, in Lincolnshire alone, one became a sink for a kitchen, another a fire-back, a cistern-bottom, hearthstone, stile in the churchyard, pair of stairs (this by the parson), a bridge.[5]

---

[1] Collier; Ecclesiastical History, VI, pp. 256, 257.
[2] State Papers, LX, No. 77. (Church Review, 14 July, 1866.)
[3] Milbourn's History of the Church of St. Mildred, Poultry, p. 40.
[4] Essex Church Goods, edited by Mr. King: Essex Archæological Society's Transactions.
[5] Peacock; Lincolnshire Church Furniture, pp. 65, 166, 112, 152. 141, 147, 150, and 65.

Some stone altars were re-erected in the reign of Queen Mary, and an Act of Parliament for the punishment of sacrilegious acts connected with them was passed in 1553;[1] an Act of Parliament was passed in 1603, forbidding their introduction from abroad;[2] others were re-erected in the Laudian period, under King Charles I, as at Durham and Worcester Cathedrals;[3] and many bishops, observing in their visitations the want of ecclesiastical propriety and decorum, issued Injunctions on the subject to the several parishes in their dioceses, some of which are printed, and particulars of others may be found amongst the State Papers in the Record Office.[4]

But this course was naturally extremely obnoxious to the Puritan party, who no sooner acquired full sway than they passed a Parliamentary Ordinance in the year 1643 (the same year in which civil marriages were introduced and enjoined), directing that all altars and tables of stone should be utterly taken away and demolished; all communion tables removed from the east end into the body of the church; all rails taken away, and also all tapers, candlesticks and basins, and all crucifixes, crosses, images, pictures, and superstitious inscriptions. But it was noted that this ordinance was not to apply to any image, picture, or arms of any king, prince, nobleman, or other dead person *not reputed or taken for a saint.*[5] At Langley, otherwise Rokely Chapel, Salop, this arrangement still subsists, or did so in 1857: the holy table being set long-wise in the midst of the choir, surrounded by a higher, sloping desk, and a kneeling-board on the north, east, and south sides; the priest presumably standing on one side.[6] And I have already adverted to the case of Deerhurst, Gloucestershire, where the chancel is still fitted with an open pew, or range of

---

[1] Act 1 Mary, 2 sess., c. 3. (See Gibson ; Codex).
[2] 3 James I, c. 5.
[3] The Smarden parish accounts for the year 1557 note the payment of 8d. "For havinge-in the altare stone out of the strete." (Archæologia Cantiana, IX, p. 233.)
[4] Some very interesting extracts from the latter were printed in the Church Review in 1869 and 1870.
[5] Scobell ; Acts and Ordinances, pp. 53, 54.
[6] Anastatic Drawing Society, 1857.

undivided stalls, running round the north, east, and south sides
of the chancel, in the midst of which stands the altar, now set
altar-wise.

SOLEMNITIES.

It is proper to mention a rubrical ceremony of washing the
altars annually with wine and water. On Maunday Thursday,
after compline and the benediction of water, two priests of the
higher grade, with deacon and subdeacon of the second rank,
and a taper-bearer of the first rank, all habited in albes and
amices, beginning with the high altar, washed all the altars
with wine and water poured out upon them; the choir mean-
while singing the responsary, "In Monte Oliveti," and in
each case, at the last washing, "Circumdederunt me," with its
versicle.[1]

The use of the altar for the purpose of giving very special
solemnity to any act may be noted; thus, in ancient times, the
Emperor of Germany was at his consecration set upon the high
altar of Maintz Cathedral, and the pope was seated on the
high altar of St. Peter's after his election. So we may refer
to Harold placing his hand upon the altar to add solemnity to
his oath.[2] In Wihgtred's Dooms Ecclesiastical, A.D. 696,[3] it
is ordered that if a man gives freedom to a slave at the altar
let the family be free: and it adverted also to the purgation
of accused of various ranks, thus: let the priest purge himself by his own veracity by saying thus, in his holy vestment,
before the altar, "I say the truth in Christ; I lie not;" the
deacon in like manner; the clerk with one hand on the altar,
the earl, the king's thane, and the common man in like manner.

In the liturgical ceremonies upon the consecration of the
queen (or king) of England (which are essentially unaltered
from the time of King Ethelred), there are presented at the
altar the queen's first oblation, consisting of an altar-cloth of
gold, and an ingot of solid gold weighing a pound: the regalia

---

[1] Sarum Missal.
[2] Represented in the nearly contemporary Bayeux tapestry.
[3] Wihgtred; Dooms Ecclesiastical, ss. 6 and 18. (Johnson; Canons.)

are placed upon the altar, as also the spurs; then the sword of state is offered there and afterwards redeemed at a price; the cross, orb, and crown are also laid upon the altar. At the offertory the queen, at the steps of the altar, takes off her crown, and makes an oblation of bread and wine which are received by the archbishop and reverently placed upon the altar; and then she makes what is called the second oblation, consisting of a purse of gold.[1]

At Kingston-on-Thames, upon the occasion of a lease being granted in the year 1203 by the men of Suberton (Surbiton, a hamlet of Kingston) to the canons of Merton Priory, a premium for the lease was paid in Kingston Church in the presence of the parishioners, and the counterpart of the lease was delivered to the Subertonians on the altar.[2] From the thirteenth century, a salmon was presented on the high altar of Westminster Abbey in commemoration of the acquisition of rights of fishery in the Thames. At St. Paul's Cathedral, until the time of Queen Elizabeth, there was annually offered before the altar a doe in winter and a buck in summer, garlanded with roses and flowers, in acknowledgment of a grant of land by the chapter. In like manner a stag was offered at Durham by the Neville family, and at York Minster a lamb by the tenants; while at Leon in Spain, each year on the 27th August, there was presented a quarter of a bull that had been killed in the last bull-fight.[3]

---

[1] Coronation Service (reprinted in Phillimore's Ecclesiastical Law, p. 1074).
[2] Cartulary of Merton Priory; Cotton MS., Cleopatra, C. vii, No. 84, fol. lxxxix, v.
[3] Walcott; Glossary.

ADJUNCTS, FURNITURE, AND ORNAMENTS

OF THE

ALTAR.

The natural belief in the existence of a Supreme Being to be worshipped and honoured, subsisting in the breasts of all men, in all ages, and demonstrating itself in every variety of religious form, has led to man's devotion of his wealth or of himself to the worship and honour of that Being ; and, since Christianity is the noblest and most ennobling form of religious belief, we may reasonably suppose that Christians were of all men most likely to show their devotion to their God by the gift to His service of that which was most precious. And so we find most marvellous proofs of such self-sacrifice throughout the history of Christianity, from the earliest period to the present. Let us note the gifts of the Emperor Constantine and the Empress St. Helena when, in the year A.D. 320, the body of St. Peter was deposited in the Basilica at Rome, and over the shrine was placed a cross of pure gold weighing 150 lbs. They gave to the Church an altar of silver enamelled with gold, and ornamented with gems to the number of 210, and weighing 350 lbs. ; 3 chalices of gold, each ornamented with 45 gems, green and blue, and each weighing 12 lbs. ; a paten of pure gold, with a tower and a dove, and adorned with gems and pearls to the number of 215, and weighing 30 lbs. ; 2 gold cruets, each weighing 10 lbs. ; a vase for incense, of the purest gold, with 51 gems, and weighing 15 lbs.; 20 silver chalices, each weighing 10 lbs.; 5 silver patens, each of 15 lbs. ; 5 silver cruets, each of 3 lbs. ; 2 silver measures, weighing 200 lbs. To these we have to add

a candelabrum 10 feet high, with 4 imitation gold candlesticks
with silver incrustations representing the Acts of the Apostles;
a gold corona in the form of a beacon, with 50 dolphins
serving as lamps, and of the weight of 35 lbs.; 32 lamps in
the choir, with dolphins, and each of 10 lbs.; and at the right
of the altar 30 silver lamps, each weighing 8 lbs.[1] From this
date we might form a series of wonderful records of munificence, till in our own time we note the church of All Saints',
Margaret Street, erected and decorated at vast cost, chiefly
by Mr. Beresford-Hope; the restoration of the Cathedral of
Christ Church, Dublin, by the late Mr. Guinness, at a sum, I
believe, of about £160,000 ; and the glorious chapel of Keble
College, built by Mr. Gibbs : works of imperial munificence
by private individuals.

Naturally, the richest materials and choicest workmanship
were lavished upon the altar and the sacred vessels and the
adjuncts, as being especially dedicated to the most solemn of
all purposes to which earthly things can be put : and in the
absence of wealth men gave to the worship of God the best
they had.   In treating of them I propose first to advert to the
coverings of the altar, and to its reredos and surroundings, and
then to the sacred vessels devoted to the service of the altar.

THE FRONTALS AND COVERINGS OF THE ALTAR.

The earliest covering seems to have been a cloth spread
upon it and hanging down on all sides, such as we should speak
of as a table-cloth,[2] as in our illustration (p. 28) from the mosaic
at San Vitale, Ravenna, which church was consecrated by
St. Maximinianus, A.D. 547.   The altar seems to have been, in
all ages, covered during the celebration of the holy mysteries,
and the practice of having three cloths, one over the other, is

---

[1] Parker ; Archæology of Rome, XI (Church and Altar Decorations),
p. 64.   Chancellor Harington (Consecration of Churches) mentions these
things more briefly, and refers for his authority to Fleury, Bk. VIII,
c. 20.
[2] In Lacroix' Military and Religious Life in the Middle Ages, English
Ed., p. 277, is an engraving of one dating in the ninth century.

said to have existed from the time of Pope Pius II: the upper one was sometimes, as in our Coronation Service,[1] called the pall. Constantine the Great gave a pall of cloth of gold

ALTAR REPRESENTED IN A MOSAIC AT SAN VITALE, RAVENNA, DATING A.D. 547.

to the Basilica of St. Peter at Rome.[2] At first, indeed, when the altar stood upon legs or brackets, or supports of a kindred nature, frontals would have scarcely been accordant, but when the altar became solid, or solid in appearance, the need of ornament was at once evident, and with the exception of those cases (which until within the last three centuries never seem to have been common abroad and very rarely, if ever, occurred here), where the stone front was carved with niches and sculpture, it was supplied by a moveable covering, in England called the frontal or tabula, in Italy the paliotto, in the Roman Missal the pallium, and sometimes in modern usage the antependium. Originally it was carried round the sides as well as front.[3] Moveable frontals were, from the fact of their moveability, peculiarly well suited to mark the Church's seasons of fast or feast. I should say, roughly, that they became usual about the year 1000, but I am not aware of any authority to whose judgment I can refer in corroboration.

---

[1] Phillimore, Ecclesiastical Law, p. 1074.
[2] Walcott, s. v. "Pall."
[3] Rock; Church of our Fathers, I, p. 236, note.

Every kind of substantial material was available: gold, silver, and baser metal gilt were frequent, though embroidery was by far more usual, and even glass and straw were not inadmissible. It will readily be supposed that frontals as well as sacred vessels were very liable to destruction from acts of sacrilege, for their fame was known far and wide, and in a case of pillage of a captured town they could hardly escape; or even for the relief of distress, as we read that St. Ambrose sold the sacred vessels in order to apply the proceeds towards the redemption of captives; or when the community of the church to which they belonged were themselves reduced to dire want; or at times when funds were most urgently needed for the ransom of the town or city. It is therefore no wonder that but few rich frontals of an early date have come down to our time. I will note the most important of those with which I am acquainted.

At Milan, in the Church of San Ambrogio, is one that is clearly of very early date. It is of silver, and covers the front, back, and ends; the front has a centre compartment, containing a rich cross between the evangelistic emblems, on either side of which are nine compartments, representing scenes in our Lord's earthly life; at the ends are raised crosses, ornamented with jewels and enamels; in the back are four circles, containing respectively figures of St. Gabriel, St. Michael, Angelbertus presenting the altar to St. Ambrose, and the latter giving him his blessing. Borders and spaces are filled in with gems and enamels, and include the name of the artist —Wolsinus magister et Phaber. Bishop Angelbertus died in 861.[1]

Basle possessed the gold frontal[2] represented in our frontispiece: it was sold by auction to a Swiss gentleman, and ultimately found its way to the Hôtel Clugny, at Paris. It is dated 1019. In the centre is represented our Lord standing, giving a benediction with the right hand while the left holds a disc and labarum; small figures crouch at the feet in lowly adoration; there are large

[1] Webb; Continental Ecclesiology, p. 208.
[2] See frontispiece.

effigies of SS. Michael, Gabriel, Rafael, and St. Benedict, besides designs of smaller size and rich borders. It appears from an ancient document that by order of the chapter this "*tabula aurea*" was to be used only on the festivals of the Nativity, Easter, Pentecost, Corpus Christi, Henry the Emperor (the donor), the Assumption, Dedication, and All Saints.[1]

In the Chapel of St. James, in the Duomo of Pistoia, is a magnificent specimen, dated 1316, with wings dated respectively 1347 and 1361; the whole is of silver, the frontal measuring 6 feet 7 inches and the sides 3 feet 5 inches, all by 3 feet 6 inches high. Even the reredos, 7 feet high, is of silver-gilt, of various dates of execution. The design of the frontal is in three tiers; in the upper tier the centre is occupied by the representation of our Lord enthroned, within an aureole, on either side of which are SS. Mary, John, and others, the Annunciation, Salutation, and Nativity, the three kings on horseback, three shepherds on camels, and the adoration of the Magi; in the middle and lower tiers are scenes from our Lord's history; on the dexter wing are the Creation, fall, and expulsion, and the like; on the sinister, scenes from the life of our Lord, and in connection with the history of St. Peter. The framework bordering the frontal and forming the division between the scenes is of a beautiful leaf pattern, with discs of translucent enamel; and the design and execution are admirable.

The high altar of Monza Cathedral has a large example in silver-gilt repoussé work, representing in the centre our Lord's baptism by St. John, between the evangelic emblems and four prophets, and around are a number of scenes in the life of St. John the Baptist. The work is somewhat rude, but the compartments are marked out by framework borders of rich, translucent enamels. A long inscription states it to be the work of Magister Borginus de Puteo, begun in 1450, and finished and placed there by his own hand on the Feast of the Decollation of St. John, seven years later.[2]

---

[1] Descriptive Pamphlet, with illustration.
[2] Archæological Journal, XIV, p. 22; by Mr. W. Burges.

1364 is the date of the magnificent silver frontal of the
high altar at St. Mark's, Venice. It is a very beautiful work,
parcel gilt, but the general design is somewhat formal, being
chiefly two tiers of statuettes in very high relief, in niches,
thirteen in a row, the upper representing our Lord, with the
Apostles on either hand, and the lower has St. Mark in the
centre, between male and female saints. The dimensions are
14 feet 2½ inches by 3 feet 3 inches. It must be noted that
this is not the celebrated Pala d'oro, which is a reredos and
is mentioned a little further on.

Beneath the Volto Santo of Lucca, by which our king,
William Rufus, usually swore, the altar and all its furniture
of the present chapel were made in 1484, of silver gilt, except a
gold lamp, weighing 24 lbs., suspended before it.

After these magnificent examples of the silversmith's art,
we may note a very remarkable frontal in one of the chapels
of Salerno Cathedral, constructed of ivories, each carved with
the utmost delicacy; they date from the fourteenth and early
in the fifteenth centuries, and if sold separately would realise
little less than their weight in gold. At Venice, several minor
altars have frontals of coloured straw, inlaid in patterns, and
by no means unsuitable in appearance, though rather too
bright, and there is one of glass in precisely similar work.

Very little research would be needed to refer to glorious
frontals of gold and silver, enriched with precious gems and
enamels, formerly existing in this as well as other countries, but
the ordinary use in the northern half of Europe was to have
frontals woven with gold thread, often enriched with gems, and
commonly wrought in embroidery, and these were unrivalled
for richness of design and material and skilful work. The
changes of sentiment which took possession of Europe in the
middle of the sixteenth century led to the destruction of most of
them, and the barbarous taste of the Renaissance period and
the still viler and more barbarous perceptions of the eighteenth
century, caused yet greater destruction; and we cannot wonder
that frontals dating earlier than the sixteenth century are
extremely rare. Good old vestments are scarce (especially if
unmutilated), though examples may be found in the treasuries

of many cathedrals in France and Germany, but frontals are
much rarer. The number which the cathedrals and larger
churches possessed was very great: at Salisbury there were
about forty, and at Durham there would appear to have been
seventy-two. At the parish church of Chipping Barnet, the
Edwardian Commissioners found " xj. alter clothes, bettar and
worse :" of which they left for the church (with unusual libe-
rality) two of the best and two of the worst.[1]

The designs of the embroidery of frontals and also of
Eucharistic vestments was frequently, as it seems to us,
singularly inappropriate, and, if I may venture to say so
without unnecessarily trespassing on the debated question of
ecclesiastical colours, nothing could be more various in hue.
A few instances will suffice. The Inventory of the Church
Goods of Westminster Abbey in 1388 mentions

> j frontellum de armis Anglie et Francie in rubeo et blodio
> velvecto, cum leopardis et floribus deliciarum contento, de
> sepultura Edwardi III.[2]

In Salisbury Cathedral was one of red samite embroidered
with lions, and another, the gift of King Edward, of white
silk with elephants.[3] Amongst the goods of the Guild of St.
Mary of Boston, was one wrought with birds and greyhounds
of gold on white damask, with eagles standing upon books,
with a scripture on their heads; one of black damask with the
arms of the donor, Mr. John Robinson, in the midst; and one
of red, powdered with pea-hens.[4] The Duchess of York, in
1495, bequeathed to her son Humphrey, two frontals of blue
damask.[5] At Westminster Abbey was one of white damask
with eagles. In a chapel out of the cloister of Sta. Maria
Novella, Florence (built 1325), is one which the Rev. B. Webb
thought the most beautiful he had ever seen ; on cloth of gold
is embroidered the Coronation of the Blessed Virgin, and on
either side six apostles under canopies ; the super-frontal also

---

[1] Cussans ; Hertfordshire Inventories, p. 29.
[2] London and Midddlesex Archæological Transactions, V, p. 426.
[3] Rock ; Church of our Fathers, IV, pp. 102, 103.
[4] Peacock ; Lincolnshire Church Goods, p. 182.
[5] Testamenta Vetusta, p. 423.

being embroidered in subjects.[1] Tournay Cathedral has a very fine example embroidered with the Tree of Jesse, that favorite mediæval genealogy of our Lord, and dating from the fourteenth century; and at Söest, in Westphalia, is a noble specimen dating from the same century.[2] I may say, in passing, that the (Lutheran) Weissenkirche at Söest is by far the most perfect mediæval church I have ever met with : its state is not due to restoration.

In England, the frontal was one of those things which it was the duty of the parishioners to provide for the celebration of divine worship, as specified in the Canons and Constitutions of the Archdioceses of York and Canterbury in 1250, 1281, and 1305.[3] At the coronation of the present Queen, following the ancient practice, she, being at the steps of the altar, made her first oblation, which is a pall or altar-cloth of gold delivered by an officer of the wardrobe to the Lord Chamberlain, and by him, kneeling, to Her Majesty ; and an ingot or wedge of gold of a pound weight ; which the Treasurer of the Household delivered to the Lord Chamberlain, and he to Her Majesty, kneeling, who delivered them to the Archbishop; and the Archbishop, standing (in which posture he was to receive all other oblations), received from her, successively, the pall to be reverently laid upon the altar, and the gold to be received into the bason, and with the like reverence placed them upon the altar.[4]

The super-frontal is either the cloth which covers the mensa, hanging a few inches over the edge, or else the frontal on-a-small-scale which covers the predella—frequently, but irregularly, called the super-altar—the term which has been already explained ; but at an early period language had not acquired its fulness and capability of exactitude, so that it not unfrequently happens, especially in technical terms, that one word was used to designate two different things, and we

---

[1] Webb ; Continental Ecclesiology, p. 328.
[2] A full description of the latter is given by Mr. Nesbitt in the Archæological Journal, IX, p. 188.
[3] Johnson ; Canons.
[4] Coronation Service (reprinted in Phillimore's Ecclesiastical Law, p. 1074).

have not even yet a distinct English term applicable to the
low shelf or ledge which so usually stands on the top of the
altar, at the back, and is especially convenient for the standing
on it of the cross and two candlesticks (if they do not stand
on the altar itself), and the vases of flowers for which it is the
proper and the only permissible place.

CANOPY, OR BALDACCHINO.

The desire to express the special reverence which
Christians feel for their Lord's earthly throne very naturally
led to the early practice of placing above it a canopy, just as
in all lands some such practice has everywhere prevailed ;
this was called the canopy, or baldacchino, and when in
western and northern countries the canopy was abandoned,
there was substituted a rich background of curtain in the
north, and a reredos in the south-west of Europe. Thus
Michael, Emperor of the East, between the years 858 and
867, gave to the church of St. Peter, Rome, two curtains of
gold thread with peacocks worked with precious stones.[1]

The baldacchino may be described as a canopy placed
over the altar as an emblem of dignity and honour; and for
the same purpose there is one erected over the throne of the
British monarch on special state occasions, and the judges'
seats in the superior courts at Westminster possess a similar
token of honour and presidency. It usually rested on four
pillars or piers, but was occasionally bracketed out from the
wall at the back, and three sides were frequently shut in by
curtains.[2] At an early period it was by no means uncommon,
and continued so in Italy until the fourteenth and perhaps the
fifteenth century; but in England, though examples up to the
eleventh century may be found, it never seems to have been
usual, and after that date, beyond perhaps isolated examples,
they were no longer erected: in fact, we have no term in the
language conveying the meaning, except the word " canopy,"
which is of a general, not specific nature, and not ordinarily

[1] Parker ; Archæology of Rome, XI, p. 65.
[2] Ibid., p. 58.

used in ecclesiological language. The word " *baldacchino* " is exclusively Italian, and its correlative was scarcely known here until the revival of ecclesiology led to the study and occasional introduction of foreign forms. A canopy over the altar is occasionally mentioned, as in the will of John Almyngham, who in 1500 bequeathed £10, willing that there be made " a canope over the hygh awter, welle done, with our Lady and 4 aungelys and the Holy Ghost, goyng upp and down with a cheyne."[1] The Latin term " *ciborium* " was occasionally applied to the structure, when occurring in England. Dr. Rock gives an illustration of an example in use in the year 802, which had curtains hung from it, and says that on great occasions it was wreathed with garlands of evergreens and flowers.[2]

Its introduction into modern use is advocated very ably by Mr. Pullan, in his pamphlet on " The Altar and Baldacchino,"[3] and not long since there was a proposal to erect one in our Cathedral of St. Paul, where, in a building of Italian type, it would not be inappropriate.

THE REREDOS.

The Reredos formed an ornamental covering to part, or the whole of the surface of the east wall above the altar; either, as is usual in this country, of a simple form, or, as in Spain and Portugal towards the end of the fifteenth and in the sixteenth centuries, carried to the height of splendour, and covering the whole wall around and above the altar with one mass of gilt metal tabernacle-work in high relief—one great surface of canopied niches and figures; and in the next century, although no longer Gothic, the design in the style called churrigueresco was singularly rich.

---

[1] Churchwardens' Accounts of Walberswick, Suffolk. Nichols; Illustrations of Manners, &c., in Middle Ages, p. 187.

[2] Rock; Church of our Fathers, I, p. 199. It will suffice to refer to a few engravings. Ninth century—Lacroix; Military and Religious Life in the Middle Ages, p. 277. See also Parker; and Pullan. At St. John Lateran, Rome, is a very rich and elaborate example, resting on marble piers, and reaching almost as high as the nave roof.

[3] Pullan ; The Altar, Baldacchino, and Reredos.

At Oporto Cathedral, the whole east end is one exceedingly rich mass of churrigueresco work of the seventeenth century, and in one of the chapels is a great silver reredos of the same date. At Guimaraës, in Portugal, the whole east end of the choir is covered with florid Renaissance work, gilt. That at Astorga Cathedral, ascribed to a pupil of Michael Angelo, is a rich and beautiful example in the revived classic style. Leon Cathedral has the back of the reredos splendidly decorated, but perhaps in honour of a royal tomb. At Alcobaça, a chapel east of the choir apse has its end filled up to the roof with canopied niches of various forms, with demi-figures, heads and hands, and other receptacles for relics (now wanting): the material is stone, thickly gilt.

I have already adverted to silver, or silver-gilt reredosses, at Pistoia and elsewhere, but the most splendid existing example is that at St. Mark's, Venice, known as the Pala d'oro. It was wrought in 1364, and given to the church in 1408 by Pope Gregory XI. I have no doubt it was intended for a frontal, from its character, proportions, and dimensions; viz., 14 feet 2½ inches by 3 feet 3 inches; but it is used as a reredos, and rests upon pillars about three feet behind the · altar which is six inches less in length.

Reredosses of this nature do not appear to have been usual in other countries, though specimens may be found, as in the magnificent reredos at Chür, Switzerland, which is a splendid example of the finest German wood carving of the fifteenth century, a period from which until the middle of the sixteenth century Germany was specially famous for such work; and examples of tabernacle-work in stone may be found in some of our larger cathedral and monastic churches. In Italy, after the revival of the art life by Cimabue at the end of the thirteenth century, paintings seem to have been the most usual decoration, and these were ordinarily triptychs; that is to say, a large central painting as wide as the altar, and wings of half its width, which, being upon hinges, might be closed by folding back upon it like the covers of a book; the central painting was usually a single subject, and the wings were occupied by many smaller scenes or single figures. One in Durham

Cathedral is described by a writer, in 1593, as "a moste curiouse and fine table with ij leves to open and close againe . . . . The whiche table was alwaies lockt up, but onely (except) on principall daies."[1] In the fifteenth and sixteenth centuries the same arrangement seems to have been usual in the rest of Eastern Europe, but not so in ordinary parish churches in England and adjacent lands, for we find that the great east window, which was the beauty and pride of the building, came down to within two or three feet of the top of the altar, and all that was practicable in the way of a reredos was simply a curtain, not very much higher than the head of the priest, or else a very small painting; e. g., John Baret, in 1463, by his will bequeathed ten marks to the painting of the reredos and table of St. Mary's altar, at Bury, with the story of the Magnificat, and in the inner part was to be written the balladys (verses) that he had made, and the pardon which he had purchased, written there also;[2] and the churchwardens of St. Michael, Cornhill, in 1550, paid 20^d for six hooks of iron to bear the table over the high altar.[3] The dossell was the English term for the painting or curtain which occupied this position. In addition to the dossell curtains, there were (chiefly at the earlier dates) on either side transverse curtains (in mediæval times termed rydells, or costers), suspended by rings upon a rod or cord.[4] The plan of closely shutting in the altar during the celebration shows how opposed to the mediæval as well as the earlier practice of Christianity is the ultramontane idea of throwing down all screens and hindrances to sight. Pugin, apropos of this subject, says: "If religious ceremonies are to be regarded as spectacles, they should be celebrated in regular theatres, which have been expressly invented for the purpose of accommodating great assemblages of persons to hear and see well."[5]

---

[1] Rites of Durham ; Surtees Society, p. 28.
[2] Will of John Baret ; Bury Wills, p. 19 ; Camden Society.
[3] St. Michael, Cornhill ; Churchwardens' Accounts, p. 85.
[4] Illustrations may easily be found ; as, for example, in Strutt's Regal and Ecclesiastical Antiquities of England, pl. ix.
[5] Pugin ; Treatise on Rood-screens, p. 8.

The curtain, hangings, or vail—" vela," generally at the back only, but frequently also at the sides of the altar, came into use at an extremely early period. It was of cloth or silk or velvet, and plain at first, but afterwards it was embroidered with figures, and for centuries the material was chiefly obtained from Cyprus and Alexandria. It is recorded that Pope Gregory IV (elected in 827), having rebuilt the Church of St. Mark, on the Esquiline Hill at Rome, gave to it several of these vails or veils (as they were indifferently spelt), and another to the Oratory of San Georgio in Velabro.[1] Leo IV (847—857), upon rebuilding the church of SS. Quattro Coronati, gave, amongst other things, four red curtains to hang round the altar:[2] in the time of his successor, Nicholas I (857—867), Michael, Emperor of the East, gave to St. Peter's at Rome, two curtains of gold thread with peacocks worked in precious stones; and at the end of the same century Pope Stephen VI presented four veils to the basilica of Sta. Maria Maggiore, one of which is stated to have been "de Alexandrino."[3] These will suffice as examples of early use in Rome. In our own country such curtains were, in the Anglo-Saxon period, often of rich silk, white, crimson, or rose-coloured, or sometimes cloth of gold, flowered with garlands of pearls;[4] but possibly this may have been a figurative way of indicating their richness.

As the English language became consolidated, the curtains were called rydells, bankers, costers, or veils;[5] abundant references to them might be given, but a few will suffice. The will of Thomas de Dalby, Archdeacon of Richmond, in 1400, mentions the receipt of vs. *pro albis curtyns pro altari in Quadragesima.*[6] In 1466, Sir Wm. Boston, of Newark,

---

[1] Parker; Archæology of Rome, XI, p. 69.
[2] Ibid., p. 61.
[3] Ibid., p. 70.
[4] Rock; Church of our Fathers, I, p. 196.
[5] The word veil is also used as a covering placed on the chalice when prepared for mass, and also for coverings for the cross and images during Lent. (Walcott.)
[6] Testamenta Eboracensia; Surtees Society, III, p. 13. The colour will be noted as a difficulty in the way of formulating any strict or general rule of colours.

Chaplain, gave to the altar of the Holy Trinity, xl*s*., and adds, *volo quod ista summa expendatur in honesta clausura biforiali, circa tabulam ad altare predict?*[1] The accounts of the churchwardens of St. Michael, Cornhill, in 1459, show an expenditure of ij^d for a lyne for the *veyle atte the high awter ;* and in 1461, *for amendyng of a rydell afore the high aucter,* iiij^d; but these may relate to a veil before the altar in time of Lent, such as that mentioned in the same accounts in 1557, when the churchwardens paid *for a vaill befor the high altar this lente* xx*s.* iiij*d.*[2]

At the Church at Söest, to which I have already adverted as retaining its mediæval fittings in singular completeness, many of the minor altars, which are simply enclosed with a low iron rail, have side curtains.

Curtains were of various colours; those at Westminster Abbey, at the dissolution, comprised blue, red, white, green, black, crimson, and changeable colours (*i. e.*, shot).[3]

Altar-curtains were hung on rods projecting from the east wall, the rings being sometimes of silver, as is believed to have been the case at Alfold, Surrey, where, temp. Edward VI, " Sertyne rynges of silver sollde for vij*s.*, the which money was bestowid in bowes and arrowes to serve the kinge."[4]

Canopy bells are mentioned, but probably for the canopy on taking the Host to the sick.

SUPER-ALTAR.

The term " Super-altar " is used in more senses than one; it more properly, perhaps, means the altar-portatile or consecrated slab, which was placed upon a table or other unconsecrated place, but in late times it was frequently applied to the shelf or ledge which stands upon and at the back of the altar, and which

---

[1] Testamenta Eboracensia, II, p. 283.
[2] Churchwardens' Accounts of St. Michael, Cornhill (privately printed by Mr. Alfred J. Waterlow).
[3] Westminster Inventory; London Archæological Transactions, vol. IV.
[4] Surrey Church Inventories; edited by J. R. Daniel-Tyssen, Esq., p. 36.

the Arches Court, in modern times, declared to be admissible, provided that it was not affixed to the mensa so as to prevent the fair linen cloth from covering the table; and probably it was this which is referred to in the accounts of the church-wardens of St. Lawrence, Reading, who in 1515[1]

> paid to a suffragan for hallowing of the high awt', Seynt
> John's awt̃, & a supʳ altre .   .   .   .   .   . vjs. viijd.

In a *Nominale* of the fifteenth century, it is explained as "a hye awtyr:"[2] evidently confusing it with the superior or high altar of the church.

This shelf was covered with a super-frontal to correspond with the frontal of the altar itself; as, for example, at St. Mary-at-Hill. "A frontell for the schelffe standyng on the altar of blue sarsenet with brydds (birds) of golde."[3]

In Italy it is called the *predella*, but the same term is quite as often used to refer to the row of small scenes which usually occupied a foot or so of painted panelling at the foot of the great altar-painting, in the nature of a reredos, so customary there from the fifteenth century.

ORNAMENTS.

It is necessary to remark expressly, that the period of introduction or use of particular items of altar ornaments or furniture can only be stated generally, for such things were not introduced or used pursuant to canons of any general Council of the church, and rarely even of any provincial synod; and, therefore, it by no means follows that because certain vessels were in use, or practices followed very gene-rally at a particular time and place, that the same was the case at other places at the same time; it may have begun later or earlier, or never been introduced there at all. The boasted uniformity of the church under the papal rule must be taken

---

[1] Coates; History of Reading, p. 218.
[2] Nominale of Fifteenth Century; ed. by Thos. Wright (privately printed, 1857).
[3] Accounts of St. Mary-at-Hill, for the year 1486; Nichols; Illus-trations, p. 113.

with very wide borders, even in important matters of doctrine
as well as discipline; and in matters of ritual and unim-
portant usages or ornaments, any exact uniformity was never
attempted or expected until within a very recent period of
Christianity; nor would it be desired by an enlightened view
of the requirements of differing peoples at different periods.

At a very early date in the history of Christianity in
western Europe, there was little or nothing left standing on
the altar when not needed during the celebration of the Holy
Sacrament; the cross, chalice and paten, and candlesticks,
seem usually to have been placed there when wanted, and
removed afterwards; but probably no fixed custom prevailed.
Our best authorities in such matters are the early mosaics
still remaining, especially at Ravenna and Rome. Gerbert
draws attention to the illuminations of the St. Blas Missal, of
the ninth century, as showing the altar "planum quidem, ac
omnibus hactenus recensitis ornamentis destitutum, vestitum
tamen;" and such was the case at Angers Cathedral up to 1718.[1]
According to Dr. Rock, the cross always stood upon the altar
in Anglo-Saxon times,[2] but Mr. Walcott states that before
the thirteenth century no candles or crosses were permitted
to be permanently set on altars, but were invariably brought
in by two acolytes when mass was to be said.[3] The representations which we meet with in illuminations and sculpture
cannot be deemed conclusive, since in such cases the altar is
represented as in use on the special occasion which forms the
subject of the work; but we generally observe a cross (not a
crucifix), a chalice and paten, and a pair of candlesticks, and
sometimes a book, or a pax, but never all together at an early
date, and each may occur alone. A few examples will suffice.

---

[1] Gerbert, I, p. 199. De Moleon; Voyages Liturgiques (quoted in
Lay Folks' Mass Book, notes by Canon Simmons; Early English Text
Society).

[2] Rock; Church of Our Fathers, I, p. 269.

[3] Walcott; Sacred Archæology, s. v. "Altar." Perhaps he was generalis-
ing from a special case; the description seems too specific for general
use. It is the great misfortune of Mr. Walcott's works that he rarely
gives exact references to any authority, and his own writings were too
extensive and numerous for exact accuracy.

An illumination to a manuscript, drawn in the ninth century,
shows a priest censing an altar covered with a table-cloth, and
on it are a chalice, wafer, and cross ; over it is a baldacchino,
and there are curtains, lamp, and bell, near.[1] In a painting
discovered a few years since in the venerable Church of San
Clemente, Rome, supposed by Father Mullooly to date from
the ninth century, but probably not earlier than the year 1100,
a priest vested for mass is standing beside an altar on which
are a chalice, paten, and book.[2] In a woodcut of the Mass of
St. Gregory, as represented in a block-book dating in the
earlier part of the fifteenth century, there are on the altar a
chalice and paten and a book.[3] A single candlestick is the
only thing standing on the altar in a xylographic " History of
the Cross," dated in 1483.[4] In the first edition of the Bible
in the French language, without date but in type of the
earliest character, is a representation of King Solomon kneeling before an altar on which are a chalice with semi-globular
cover, a standing monstrance, a smaller covered vessel, a
paten, a round box (probably for wafers), and a maniple.[5] In
an edition of the Legenda Aurea, printed at Lyons in 1486,
in a woodcut representing St. Lupus communicating King
Clothair (with a wafer), the altar has on it only a chalice and
two small candles ; the reredos is a rood with SS. Mary and
John in high relief.[6] In an edition of the Legenda Aurea,
published in 1519, an illustration shows an altar with only a
crucifix on it.[7] It may be well to mention the custom in the
mediæval period of representing in works of art the costume
and detail of the period of execution, without regard to what
they were or were supposed to have been at the date of the
scene represented.

[1] Engraved in Lacroix' Military and Religious Life in the Middle Ages,
p. 277.
[2] Marriott ; Vestiarium Christianum, pl. xliii. Mullooly ; Painting at
San Clemente, Rome, 4to, 1866.
[3] Livres Xylographiques ; Berjeau, p. 82.
[4] History of the Cross ; fac-simile reprint, edited by Berjeau.
[5] La Bible en Francoiz, Tome II, ffeuillet xviii.
[6] Legenda Aurea, Lyons, folio, 1486, fol. cxxiii.
[7] Legenda Aurea, 1519, fol. ccxii.

In the *Capitula* issued in the year 994 by Theodulph, Archbishop of Canterbury, it was forbidden to use the church as a storehouse for corn or hay or other worldly goods, but that nothing should be kept there but the holy books, the housel vessels, and the mass vestments, and the general furniture of the church.[1]

The vessels and ornaments required for the altar are specified amongst the things which the parishioners were bound to provide for their church for use in divine service, as distinguished from those for which the rector was responsible, in the York Constitutions of Archbishop Gray in 1250, and afterwards in the Canterbury Statutes of Archbishop Peckham, c. 1281, and again in the Constitutions of Merton, under Archbishop Winchelsea in 1305, which are almost identical with those of Archbishop Gray.[2] There are specified the chalice, pyx, pax, and books, and a frontal for the high altar. Cross and candlesticks are not mentioned, though a cross for processions and an Easter taper and candlestick are specified, and a censer is inserted in the Orders of 1281. We must presume that these other items were included in the residue which the rector was bound to provide.

THE CHALICE AND PATEN.

First then, as to the chalice and paten. Upon them, as was most natural and laudable, every treasure of material and workmanship was lavished. In the year 320, in the great festival held upon the occasion of the body of St. Peter being deposited in the Basilica of St. Peter, at Rome, the Emperor Constantine and the Empress St. Helena presented, amongst other things (as previously more fully detailed), 3 chalices of gold with gems, green and blue, each having 45 jewels and weighing 12 lbs.; also 20 silver chalices each weighing 10 lbs.; a paten of pure gold, with a dove adorned with gems, green and blue, and white pearls numbering 215, and weighing 30 lbs.; and 5

---

[1] *Capitula* of Theodulph, A.D. 994. (Johnson ; Canons.)
[2] Johnson ; Canons.

silver patens, each weighing 15 lbs.[1] In the next century, Pope
Hilary (461–7) gave to the same cathedral 10 silver chalices,
each of the weight of 7 lbs.[2] At Kremsmünster is the oldest
chalice existing in Germany, having been presented by the
founder of the church in the year 777 ; it is of copper with niello
and gold ornaments.[3] In the next century, Pope Pascal I (817)
gave to the Church of St. Cecilia, in Trastevere, 26 silver
chalices, together weighing 109½ lbs. Michael, Emperor of
the East, presented to the Church of Rome a paten of pure
gold with precious stones, white, green, and blue, and a gold
chalice with gems set about it.[4] It would be needless to note
examples of the value of chalices and patens from that date
downwards to the present time. Rock states that in the
Anglo-Saxon period they were frequently of the purest gold
and sparkling with jewels ;[5] and, subsequently, we have
abundant records of similar gifts by kings and nobles.[6]

Where means and devotion permitted, the royal metal,
gold, was appropriated to this use, but such of course could
rarely be the case. Next came silver, as in the instances
already noted ; it was frequently gilt, and its habitual use has
continued generally down to the present day ; and where
means would not permit of making the whole chalice of that
metal the bowl was silver. But where poverty prevented this,
various other materials were used, and restrictive canons from
time to time were made to prevent the serious irreverence and
accident which might otherwise have been occasioned.

Glass was frequently used at an early date ;[7] in the
catacombs at Rome have been found parts of glass cups,
enamelled in gold, with subjects which leave no doubt of their

---

[1] Parker ; Archæology of Rome, XI, pp. 64, 65.
[2] Ibid., p. 21.
[3] Lubke ; Ecclesiastical Art in Germany, p. 140.
[4] Parker ; Archæology of Rome, XI, p. 65.
[5] Rock ; Church of our Fathers, I, p. 269.
[6] E. g., John, Duke of Exeter, by his will, 16th July, 1447, bequeathed
a chalice of gold, with the whole furniture of his chapel, to the Church
of St. Katherine, beside the Tower of London. (Nichols ; Testamenta
Vetusta, p. 255.)
[7] Bingham ; Christian Antiquities, p. 109.

having been intended for chalices;[1] but the material was discouraged from fear of accident. An instance is mentioned in the Legenda Aurea, where, at the Church of St. Lawrence, Milan, a deacon was carrying to the altar a crystalline chalice of wonderful beauty, when it slipped from his hands and was broken to fragments; but the worthy deacon collected the fragments and placed them upon the altar of St. Lawrence and prayed, and the broken chalice was made whole and taken up consolidated.[2]

In the Fasciculus Temporum it is stated that Pope Zepherinus, in the year 204, ordered that the vessels of the altar should be (at least) of glass or tin, and not of wood as had been done in old time.[3]

Honorius III (pope from 1216 to 1227) addressed the Bishop Berxineñ (? Brixen), commanding him to deprive the priest of the Church of St. Bridget in that place, for having *in pane fermentato, cipho ligneo missar° solemnia celebrare presumpsit.*[4]

In Anglia, in the tenth century, to such poverty were the people reduced by the frequent incursions of the Danes, that Ælfric issued the following, amongst other canons, in the year 957.[5] The priest

> shall have his mass vestment, that he may reverently minister to God, as is becoming; and let not that vestment of his be sordid, at least not to the sight: and his altar cloths well made. Let his chalice be made of pure wood, not subject to rottenness; and also the paten: and let the corporal be clean so as befits Christ's ministration. A thing of this sort is not to be treated without great care; but he shall be ever honoured with God who ministers to Him in wisdom and purity.

In Lanfranc's Canons, made at Winchester in 1071, it was ordered that chalices should not be made of wax or

---

[1] Maitland; Church in the Catacombs. Northcote on the Catacombs.
[2] Legenda Sanctorum: ed. Lyons, 1486, fol. cxii.
[3] Fasciculus Temporum: Venice, 1479.
[4] Decretals of Pope Gregory IX, p. 442.
[5] Johnson; Canons.

wood.[1] In 1175, the Council of Rheims directed they should
be of gold or silver, and that no bishop should bless a chalice
of tin, and the Constitutions of the Province of Canterbury,
held in the same year under Archbishop Richard, adopted it;[2]
but there seems a doubt how far this order was enforced.
The Legatine Constitutions of York direct that it should
be of silver, where means would permit. This direction was,
however, of an exceptional nature, and its very wording
shows that there existed a necessity for permitting what
otherwise was undesirable. And we find that by the laws of
Northumbrian priests in 950 they were forbidden, under a
heavy fine, to consecrate the housel in a wooden chalice.[1]
In the canons enacted in the time of King Edgar, c. 960, it
was ordered that every chalice should be molten, and *not* of
wood.[1] By the Legatine Canons of Cealchythe, in 795, it
was expressly forbidden that the chalice or paten should be of
ox-horn.[1]

In the York Canons, in 1195, under Bishop Hubert
Walter, it was ordered that the Eucharist be consecrated in a
silver chalice, where there was a sufficiency (of funds) for it.[3]
By the Constitutions of Archbishop Langton, in 1222, it
was ordained that every church have a silver chalice, with
other decent vessels, and the archdeacon was directed to take
care that the ornaments of the altar should be decent.[4]

Practically, the richest and most valuable materials and
workmanship, within the means of the donor, were devoted to
this purpose; and among these we find onyx, sardonyx, agate,
and ivory, mentioned by early French writers, and marble by
Gregory the priest;[5] of which a few instances will suffice.
John, Duke of Exeter, in 1447, bequeathed to the Church of
St. Katherine, beside the Tower (of London), a chalice of
gold, with the furniture of his chapel.[6] Bishop William of
Wykeham bequeathed to the altar at his place of sepulture a

---

[1] Johnson ; Canons.
[2] Ibid. ; and Lyndwood.
[3] Johnson ; Canons.
[4] Ibid. ; and see Lyndwood, p. 249.
[5] Walcott.
[6] Testamenta Vetusta, p. 255.

gold chalice, with *uno pari urceolorum* (presumably cruets), one pair of candlesticks, a bell, and a pax of gold, besides silver articles.[1] At Westminster Abbey, at the time of the dissolution, there were amongst other things a golden chalice weighing 14 oz., and seven chalices of silver and gilt weighing 167 oz.[2]

The abundance of plate expressly for use in divine worship which secular persons possessed seems singular at the present date, and can only be partially accounted for by the multitude of private chapels attached to churches, supplemented by the private chapels of mansions ; a reminiscence of the latter is preserved in the right of every nobleman to have a domestic chaplain. And, beyond the gift of chalices which testators possessed, they frequently directed that others should be supplied to favourite churches or chapels ; thus Humphrey de Bohun, Earl of Hereford and Essex, in 1361 in his will says :—

> Nous volons auxint et devisoms ℔ nos executours facent faire xiij. chalys en noun de Dieux et de ses douce apostres (nom de Dieu et de ses douze apôtres), et v. chaliz d'argent en noun de v. joyes de Nôtre Dame, et qu'ils les facent ailler as diverses esglises poevres, à chescune esglise un chaliz, si ℔ nous soions en les proiers de genz conversanz as dite esglese à touz jours.[3]

It would appear, therefore, from what has been said, that from the end of the tenth century metal was invariably used, up to the time of King Edward VI when various churches were, by his commissioners, or by independent sacrilege, denuded of all that had a money value so completely, that when his second set of commissioners went round in his sixth and seventh year to sweep up the crumbs which their predecessors had missed or thought beneath their notice, we learn that in default of silver, glass and even wooden chalices were in use : where a chalice had been left it was the second best. A few examples from the inventories made by the commissioners will suffice for illustrations. At Lawling, Essex, the churchwardens reported that they had laid out 4ˢ 4ᵈ for a

---

[1] Nichols ; Royal Wills, p. 324.
[2] London and Middlesex Archæological Transactions, IV, p. 371.
[3] Nichols ; Royal Wills, p. 50.

Communion table, and 2ᵈ for a glass ; and the commissioners
appointed to the churchwardens "for the admynistracōn
wᵗin the same, the said glasse, the cope, the surples, and the
towels," while at the same time they reserved to the king's
use the only object of even the smallest pecuniary value, viz.,
a silver chalice weighing 4 oz. At Tillingham, in the same
county, was a glass which served for the Communion cup.
At Offley, Hertfordshire, the churchwardens reported to the
commissioners that "their chalise was stollen, and now they
m'stre wᵗ a glas."[1]   At Denge, they appointed to the church
" the worste of the ij. challyces," and the same was done in at
least seven cases in Hertfordshire.[2]   In the king's first year
there had been sold of the church goods at Stambridge a silver
chalice, parcel gilt, weighing 16 ounces : when the commissioners came again there remained for God's service " A cuppe
of wood for yᵉ mynistracōn," and this was redelivered to the
churchwardens for the use of the church.[3]   It is not necessary
to refer to similar cases in other countries.   There is a curious
chalice of very little later date preserved at Tong, Shropshire,
the bowl of which is glass or crystal, and the rest metal ; it
stands 12½ inches high, and has a cover.   From its appearance
I do not doubt that its original destination was for secular
purposes.[4]

At the consecration of a church it has always been, and is
still, the custom to place the chalice and paten upon the altar
and hallow them : but when necessary, they were separately
consecrated : one example, four centuries ago, will suffice, viz. :
at St. Michael's, Cornhill, in 1469, there was paid " to Maister
John Reresly, for hallowyng of a chaleys, ijᵈ," and for another
in the same year iiijᵈ.[5]   A form of benediction is given, with
music, in the Pontifical.[6]

---

[1] Cussans ; Herts Inventories, p. 62.
[2] Ibid., p 34.
[3] Essex Archæological Society's Transactions ; Inventories of Church
Goods, edited by H. W. King, Esq.   At Denge, they left several copes,
vestments, and rochets, presumably unsaleable.
[4] Anastatic Drawing Society, 1857, pl. 31.
[5] St. Michael, Cornhill, Churchwarden's Accounts, pp. 40 and 41.
[6] Pontifical ; fol., c. 1500, but sine anno et loco.

With the ritual usages connected with the chalice, and its filling and rinsing, I must not pause to deal, nor with the piscina and its use.

At an early date the form of the chalice was simply that of an ordinary goblet, the richest and most precious of which were devoted to God's service. All or nearly all the earliest chalices depicted are two-handed vases. Such is that shown in our illustration (p. 28, *ante*), from a mosaic at San Vitale, Ravenna. One dating from the sixth century was found at Gourdon.[1] One at Kremsmünster, which was the gift of the founder in 777, is of copper with niello and gold ornaments, and a band of pearls.[2] Another is represented in the illumination to a manuscript of the ninth century engraved by

CHALICE IN POSSESSION OF THE AUTHOR (PURCHASED AT ROME).

Lacroix;[3] of the tenth century is that of St. Goslin, preserved at Nancy;[4] of the twelfth century there is one, very elaborately ornamented, in the Benedictine Abbey of Wilten,

[1] Caumont; Abécédaire, woodcut, p. 66.
[2] Ibid., p. 140. Two other fine examples are engraved on pp. 139 and 140 of the same work.
[3] Lacroix; Military and Religious Life, p. 277.   [4] Caumont, p. 67.

E

near Innsbrück;[1] and an engraving of one at Tarascon, is given by Caumont.[2]

The description of the form comprises three parts, viz.: the bowl; the stem, with a knob (or knop) half-way down, to assist in the grasp as well as for ornament; and the foot or base, on which a representation of the crucifix in enamel or engraving has been customary.

The paten was equally rich with the chalice. It is made so as to fit upon the chalice and make a cover for it.

It has been thought that the date of a chalice, from the eleventh century downwards, might be told from its form, but beyond a very general indication I do not think much can be said: the details, when of a distinctive character, furnish a better indication. But so far as this we may go: the bowl in the earlier mediæval period was generally flat and shallow—a

CHALICE REPRESENTED ON A BRASS AT SHORNE, KENT, A.D. 1519.

depressed hemisphere—and the base also circular; that subsequently the bowl became deeper in proportion, and then the lower part of the section only was curved, the sides being straight-lined or nearly so, sloping outwards; and by the fourteenth century the foot had been changed to a hexagon for the convenience of a rubric which directed that the chalice should

---

[1] Lacroix, p. 233. Lubke, p. 138. [2] Caumont; Abécédaire, p. 246.

be laid down upon the paten to drain off, which might have led to inconvenience if the foot were still circular.[1]

When the cup was restored to the laity, the bowls were necessarily very much larger than they had for some centuries been made.

Church plate was so sought after by the Royal Commissioners, and "annexed" for the king's use, that even in 1549 the parish of St. Dionis, Backchurch, had to buy (as appears by the accounts) "ij coppes of sylver and gilt, waying 61 owncys at 7ˢ 4ᵈ the ownce, for the Comunyon tabyll, costing xxij*li*. vij*s*. iiij*d*."[2] Chalices of Elizabethan date are not uncommon in our English churches; they are generally very simple in design, and were, we can have little doubt, given to replace those plundered by the Edwardian Commissioners.

CORPORAL, PALL, BURSE, AND VEIL.

Other accessories were the corporal, pall, burse, and veil, but it is not very easy to define their form and use in early days, since each of these terms was also otherwise applied; it must always be borne in mind that words have not at an early period in the history of a language the same exact, definite, and limited meaning that they subsequently acquire when the language becomes fuller and richer and possesses a word expressing a particular meaning, which word is limited to that one meaning; though probably no language has yet attained to perfection in this respect.

The corporal is defined by Dr. Lee as a square piece of linen, on which is placed the "Corpus" during the Holy Sacrifice. Anciently it was much larger than it is at present. St. Isidore, of Pelusium, in the beginning of the fifth century, compares it to the clean linen cloth in which St. Joseph of Arimathæa wrapped the body of our Lord.[3]

---

[1] There is an interesting and valuable article on this subject by Mr. Micklethwaite, in the Proceedings of the Society of Antiquaries, 2nd series, VIII, p. 155.

[2] London and Middlesex Archæological Transactions, IV, p. 205.

[3] Lee; Glossary, *s. v.* "*Corporal*."

This veil (as distinguished from the vela or curtain before referred to) is described by Dr. Lee as a covering of silk, embroidered, and of the colour of the season, used for placing over the chalice and paten when prepared for mass, and afterwards.[1] Walcott adds that in France it covered the chalice during the elevation, but not so in England.[2]

The burse is described, by the same authority, as the purse or receptacle for the corporal and chalice-cover; a square, flat receptacle, formed of cardboard covered with rich silk or cloth of gold embroidered and studded with jewels, open on one side only, and placed over the chalice veil when the sacred vessels are carried to the altar by the celebrant.[3]

The pall (on the same authority) is a piece of millboard, six to eight inches square, covered with linen and embroidered with a cross and border on the upper side, used to place over the surface of the chalice at certain portions of the mass.[4] Probably it would be a very difficult task to show at all conclusively what the article was until a modern date. Walcott states it to be another name for the corporal; as also for the linen cloth covering the mensa;[5] and in our own Coronation Service it is spoken of as of gold.

Archbishop Gray's Constitutions, in 1250, enumerate, amongst the articles which it was the duty of the parishioners to provide for their church, *tribus thuellis et corporalia*; also a Lent veil.[6]

When a church was consecrated, the sacred vessels were usually placed upon the altar and consecrated with it; but they might be separately consecrated at any time.[7] Among the injunctions to treat sacred vessels with respect, it may suffice to refer to the Canon of 994, which runs to this effect: "Let no cleric, and still less a layman, dare presume to use

---

[1] Lee; *s. v. "Veil."*
[2] Walcott; *s. v. "Veil;"* he gives other applications of the same word, such as curtains of great richness, used only in Lent.
[3] Lee; Glossary, *s. v. "Burse."*
[4] Ibid., *s. v. "Pall."*
[5] Walcott; *s. v. "Pall."*
[6] Archbishop Gray's Register, fol. 23; Surtees Society, p. 371.
[7] See Pontifical.

either the cup or the dish, or any of the vessels which are hallowed to divine service, for any worldly purpose. Plainly, he who drinketh anything out of the hallowed cup but Christ's Blood, which is consecrated in the mass-song, or that puts the dish to any other service but that of the altar, he ought to consider that that concerns him, as it did Balthasar (when he had seized the vessels hallowed to the Lord, for his own use), viz., he lost at once his life and his kingdom."[1]

As to the liturgical directions respecting the chalice, it would expand the present paper too largely to include them; but I may mention that it was decided by Pope Gregory II, in answer to an inquiry by St. Boniface, that it is not fit (*congruum non est*) to place two or three chalices on the altar, *cum missarium solemnia celebrantur*.[2]

It was anciently customary at the burial of a priest to place upon his breast a chalice, which was buried with him; such chalice was probably made for the purpose, being (in the many instances where they have been found) of pewter, very plain, and so small as to be more like a model.

REED.

In early inventories we find mention of a REED, and examples of the vessel itself may, though extremely rarely, be met with; it was used, I believe, for administration of the Holy Sacrament to the sick, when it could not be given from the chalice without risk of accident; but very little indeed seems to be known about it. Dr. Rock states that it was in use in the Anglo-Saxon period and was formed of gold, silver, or tin; and he gives engravings of specimens.[3] Examples of spoons for the same purpose have been noted.

THE PYX.

The vessel in which the Holy Sacrament, in the form of bread, is reserved for the need of the sick, is so called.

---

[1] Johnson; Canons.
[2] Rock; Church of our Fathers, I, p. 165.   [3] Ibid.

Such a vessel was used for the purpose from early Christian times. By the ancient custom it was suspended over the altar, and thence sometimes spoken of as the "suspensio." The favourite form for a pyx was that of a dove, or occasionally a tower. Pyxes in the form of a dove, beautifully enamelled, may not infrequently be seen in museums abroad; there was recently and probably still is one in use at St. John's, Malta. But in the fourteenth century it was most frequently a small box, circular in form, in accordance with the form of the Host, and with a conical lid, usually

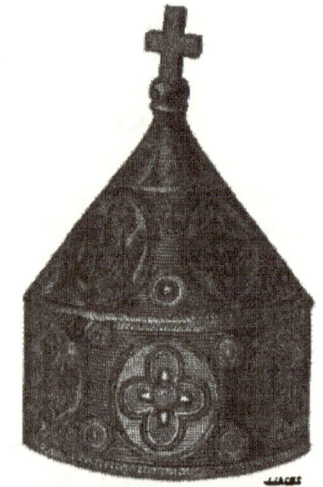

ENAMELLED PYX, IN POSSESSION OF THE AUTHOR.

terminating in a cross; it was sometimes formed of ivory, sometimes of wood, but generally of metal, often gilt within and externally enamelled. The term corporas, or corporax, seems to have been often used as a synonym for pyx, though sometimes (as the Prayer Book of Edward VI, in 1549[1]) for a cloth placed upon the paten or in the pyx, and at other times for the covering placed upon the pyx, which Walcott states was a thin veil of silk or muslin; that at Durham was of very fine lawn, embroidered with gold and red silk, and

---

[1] Rubric to Prayer Book of 1549 (Parker Society Ed., p. 85).

finished with four knobs and tassels.[1] A pyx cover is mentioned in the inventory of St. Mary-at-Hill in 1485-6[2]:—

> A pyx clothe for the high aulter, of Sipers (Cyprus) frenged with gold, with knoppes of golde and sylke, of Spayneshe makyng; of the gift of Mr. Doctor Hatclyff, parson.
>
> A pyx clothe of Sipers, frenged with grene sylke and red, with knoppes silver and gylt, with corners ; goyng of Mrēs Sucklyng's gyfte.

For such use was the bequest of John Osborne to the Church of Purleigh, Essex, in 1511[3]:—

> I bequeth my typett of sarsenett to be hanged oᵛ the pixe wᵗ the holy Sacramēt of the forsaid high aulter.

At Chipping Barnet, to take another example, was :[4]—

> A clothe of nedyll worke, and another of silke, for the pyxe.

From the latter part of the fifteenth century an important change took place; the pyx was no longer suspended, but was placed in a niche in the reredos, over the altar, and necessarily furnished with a door and a lock; and to suit this changed arrangement the pyx had a foot attached, which gave it the descriptive title of a "standing pyx;" and it took the form of a covered chalice. By this time the ciborium or baldacchino had been generally abandoned, and the term ciborium was frequently applied to a standing pyx. The original custom of a suspended pyx was never abandoned in this country, for in the reign of Queen Mary we find it mentioned frequently; as, in the Churchwardens' Accounts of St. Michael, Cornhill, "Paid for a pyxe to hange oᵛ the hye awlter, iijˢ iiijᵈ;"[5] and in 1556 they "Paide for a corde to pull upe the sacrament, iiijᵈ;"[6] and probably in many places it hung beneath a canopy, as at Durham, which is described as most sumptuous, while the pyx itself was of most pure, fine gold, curiously wrought of goldsmith's work.[7]

---

[1] Walcott, s. v. "Corporax Cups."
[2] Nichols ; Illustrations, &c., p. 114.
[3] Essex Archæological Society, 2nd Series, I, p. 172.
[4] Cussans ; Hertfordshire Inventories, p. 29.
[5] St. Michael, Cornhill ; Churchwardens' Accounts, p. 115.
[6] St. Michael, Cornhill ; Churchwardens' Accounts, p. 129.
[7] Rites of Durham ; Surtees Society, p. 7.

Such being the history of the changes which have taken place
in the pyx, I may give a little detail and a few illustrative
examples. The Legatine Constitutions, made at Westminster
in 1138, after directing that the reservation do not exceed
eight days, order that the Host be not carried to the sick
by other than a priest or deacon, though it might be by any
one in case of necessity, but still with the greatest reverence.[1]
The Canons in 1200, under Archbishop Walter, direct the
reservation in a clean, suitable pyx, which, when carried to
the sick, should have a clean cloth laid over it.[2] The Constitutions of Archbishop Edmund, in 1236, assume that it would
be conveyed only by a priest.[3] It was one of the items of
church furniture ordered by the Constitutions of Archbishop
Gray (of York) in 1251.[4] The Constitutions of Archbishop
Peckham, in 1281, direct that in every church a tabernacle,
suitable to the church and its capability, should be made for
the Sacrament of the Eucharist, wherein (not in a burse, or
" loculo," on account of risk of comminution, but in a beautiful pyx, lined with whitest cloth) It should be placed and
It should be received every Lord's day, according to the rule
of the General Council.[5] By the Canons under Archbishop
Reynolds, in 1322, it was ordered that the pyx should be
of silver, or ivory, or otherwise befitting, and the Host not
reserved above seven days.[6]

As instances of the hanging pyx, two will suffice. In the
will of Lady Margaret la Zouche, in 1449, she says: " I be-
queath a box of silver, the which hynges (hangs) in my
chapell, to y^e chirch of Kyrklington, y^t God Almyghty in y^e
forme of bred may lie in, over y^e high auter in the same
chirche;"[7] and in the same year William Bruges, Garter-
King-at-Arms, bequeathed to the Church of St. George,
Stamford, " a little round cofyn of syl$\tilde{v}$ closed-to, in synging
brede ᚁ not y^e hoste;" and also " 1 coupe of syl$\tilde{v}$, in the
which is j litel box of yvory to put in (in which to put) the

[1] Johnson ; Canons.   [2] Ibid.   [3] Ibid.   [4] Ibid.
[5] Gibson ; Codex, p. 464. See also Lyndwood, p. 248.
[6] Johnson ; Canons.
[7] Testamenta Eboracensia ; Surtees Society, II, p. 157.

blessid sacrament and to hang ov̇ the high awter whan the said chauncell is redy closed round aboute." [1]

This extract serves to call attention to an error which might easily be made with respect to boxes of a kindred, yet very distinct, use, viz., the box for "singing bread," and the pyx to contain the same after consecration. The former term was used for the box which contained the wafers ready for consecration, and the latter for that which contained the consecrated Host. The larger altar-breads, a single one of which was consecrated for consumption by the priest alone, were called "singing-breads," or "singing-cakes," and the smaller ones, which were used for communicating the people, were called "houselling-bread;" thus "houselling-folk" were persons of sufficient age to receive the Housell, and consequently a synonym for communicants at large.[2] Both vessels are shown in a wood engraving in the earliest French Bible, in which, with customary anachronism, King Solomon is represented kneeling before an altar on which are a standing pyx, a round box for the altar-breads, and other vessels.[3] At Sawbridgeworth, Hertfordshire, the Edwardian Commissioners noted [4]

A pyx of sylver and gylt, with a glasse in yt and ij lytle bells of sylver hangynge therat ; wayes altogether xxxij½ ounces.

---

[1] Will of Wm. Bruges ; Lambeth Register, 187, Stafford.

[2] The first Prayer Book of King Edward VI directed that "The Bread that shall be consecrated shall be such as heretofore hath been accustomed. And every of the said consecrated Breads shall be broken into two pieces at the least, or more, at the discretion of the minister, and so distributed. (Sparrow ; Collection, p. 23.) But the custom was subsequently changed, though restored soon afterwards, as shown by the Injunctions of Queen Elizabeth, in 1557, which give the following order : "Where also it was in the time of King Edward the Sixt used to have the Sacramental Bread of common fine bread, it is ordered, for the more reverence to be given to these holy mysteries, being the Sacraments of the Body and Blood of our Saviour Jesus Christ, that the same Sacramental Bread be made and formed plain, though somewhat bigger in compasse and thicknesse, as the usuall bread and water heretofore named 'Singing Cakes,' which served for the use of the private masse." (Sparrow ; Collection, p. 79.) Robert Burton, the author of the Anatomy of Melancholly, vicar of St. Thomas', Oxford in 1616, and rector of Segrave, Leicestershire in 1640 (Preface xvi, to ed. 1804), always used wafers ; and certainly not from any Roman tendency, as his well-known work abundantly shows.

[3] La Bible en Francoiȝ, II, ffeuillet xviii.

[4] Cussans ; Hertfordshire Church Goods, p. 116.

The final inventory of St. Stephen's Chapel, Westminster, mentions :—

> One stondyng pix of sylver & gylt to bere the Sacrament in, set w᾽ stone & perle ; by esᵗ (estimation) besides the cristall . . . vij˟˟ xj oz.
>
> Itm̄, one pix of ivcry garnyshed w᾽ sylver & gilte, by estimacion of . . . . . . iij onz., j di.
>
> A box of every with-in the pyxe, havyng smayle glasses of sylver apon hit (presumably for ornament).[1]
>
> A trinitie of sylver & gylt ; iiij aungelles of sylᵱ & gylt, & an image of oʳ lady & the holy-gost (evidently the Annunciation) ; beryng the sacramēt, of sylver & gylt, hangyng oᵱ the hie aulter, of [2] . . . . iijᶜ xvj onz., di.

The standing pyx was necessarily much more accessible than the suspended form, and it was easy for thieves to break open the tabernacle door and steal it; thus, in 1415, there was brought to the English camp in France an English robber who had stolen from a church a pyx of copper gilt (believing it to be gold,) which contained the Holy Sacrament; and, in the next village where they stopped for the night, he was hung.[3] This is the incident which Shakespeare adverts to in his play of Henry V, and will serve as an illustration of the singular exactness with which he followed the history of the Chroniclers. It will be remembered how Pistol asks the intervention of Fluellen on behalf of Bardolph:—

> *Pistol:* Fortune is Bardolph's foe, and frowns on him ;
> For he hath stol'n a pix, and hanged must 'a be.
> A damned death !
> Let gallows gape for dog, let man go free,
> And let not hemp his wind-pipe suffocate ;
> But Exeter hath given the doom of death
> For pix of little price.[4]

---

[1] Inventory of St. Stephen's Chapel, Westminster; London and Middlesex Archæological Transactions, IV, p. 371, and note *b.*
[2] Ibid., p. 373.
[3] Gesta Henrici Quinti, edited by Bcnjn. Williams (Royal Historical Society), p. 41.
[4] Henry V, Act III, scene 6.

The bombastic language (including the mixed metaphor
of gallows gaping) though so ill-suited to the rough Welsh-
man addressed, the moderate amount of energy displayed for
the benefit of his old friend and boon companion, the perfect
callousness to the offence of sacrilege, and the feeling that
the severity of the sentence was enhanced by the fact of the
pyx being of little price, furnish together one of the most
marked illustrations of Bardolph's character shown in the
play.

At St. Margaret, Westminster, a similar robbery appears
to have been effected in 1531, when, as it appears by their
accounts,[1] they

> · Paid for mette for the theff that stalle the pyx . . . iiij⁴

An Act of Parliament was passed in the third year of
King James I (cap. 5), 1605, forbidding the introduction
from beyond the seas of popish books, and authorising jus-
tices, mayors, bailiffs, and others, to search the houses of any
popish recusant convict, or one whose wife was such, and seize
such books or any altar, *pyx*, beads, &c., and destroy them, or
if there be an article of price, to deface it at the quarter
sessions and then restore it.[2]

MONSTRANCE.

The monstrance, as shown by its derivation from the word
"*monstrare*," to show, was a temporary receptacle for the
Host, for the convenience of devotional exhibition to the
congregation. It was also called an ostensorium; the standing pyx was often identical with it. The requirement arose,
according to Dr. Rock, in consequence of the institution of the
festival of Corpus Christi,[3] and monstrances were not general
before the fourteenth century. Walcott refers to Acts of the

---

[1] St. Margaret, Westminster, Accounts. (Nichols; Illustrations, p. 10.)
[2] Gibson; Codex, p. 631.
[3] The festival of Corpus Christi was instituted by Pope Urban IV in
1264, and confirmed by the Council of Vienne in 1311. It is held on the
Thursday after Trinity Sunday. (Walcott; and Haydn.)

Council of Cologne, in 1452, leading to the inference that
the Holy Sacrament had previously been usually carried in a
closed ciborium. Such would also appear from the fact that by
far the greater number of the ancient existing examples date
from the second half of the fifteenth and the sixteenth and subsequent centuries. For description, it may suffice to say that
the foot and stem resemble those of a chalice or ciborium,
while the upper part instead of a bowl has two discs of glass
or crystal set up edgewise, between the two faces of which is
a sufficient space for the Host. The exterior is usually surrounded by rays, and surmounted by tabernacle-work and
pinnacles. Riches of art and material were lavished upon it;
all that wealth could offer. Often of gold, resplendent with
jewels, and more frequently of silver, or of brass or copper
gilt, yet no material was deemed unworthy if a baser substance were enforced by the donors' want of means; and
wooden examples are ·recorded. The size varies greatly, up
to a height of five feet. A few examples may be noted. In
the will of Lord Despencer, in 1375, he left to the Abbot
and Convent of Tewkesbury [1]

> A ewer, wherein to put the Body of Christ on Corpus Christi day,
> which was given me by the King of France.

Among the goods at Westminster Abbey, in 1388, were the
following:

> Tabernaculum vetus, cum costis, de berillo cum ymaginibus in
> eisdem depictis, ornatum argento, pro Corpore Christi, antiqui-
> tus, in eodem ponendo.
>
> j Jocale magnum de berillo pro Corpore Christi imponendo, in
> argento deaurato, artificiose compositum, ex dono dom. Thome
> ducis Gloucestri.[2]

Thomas, Earl of Warwick, left to the College of Our Lady
of Warwick, amongst other things, a precious stone called a
berill,[3] bound with silver and enamelled, to put the Host

---

[1] Testamenta Vetusta, p. 99.
[2] London and Middlesex Transactions, V, p. 431.
[3] Beryll, which was very generally used for this purpose, would appear
to be rock-crystal. Pliny speaks of it as being of a sea-green colour, and
used as a material for gem engraving. Leland applies the term, in one
case, to window-glass. (Notes to Testamenta Vetusta, xx.)

into."[1] The renowned Bishop William of Wykeham, by his will, in 1403, bequeathed to the Church of Winchester " one vessel of beryll, ordained for the body of Christ."[2] John, Duke of Exeter, in 1447, bequeathed to the high altar of the Church of St. Katherine, beside the Tower of London, "a cup of byrel, garnished with gold, pearls, and precious stones, to put the Holy Sacrament in."[3] The inventories of the Church of St. Mary-at-Hill in 1431-2, mention a " cowpe of silver and gold, to lay-in Godde's body, with cristall; a cowpe of silver for Godde's body;" and in 1498 was paid a charge of 1ˢ 4ᵈ "for mendyng of the monstyr for the Sacrament."[4] At Westminster Abbey, at the dissolution, there was "a nooser" (i. e. "an ostensorium") of silver, with berall, of curious work, and weighing 144 oz.[5]

THE TABERNACLE,

In which to place the pyx, was not in use in England till five or six years before the Reformation, or until Queen Mary's reign,[6] notwithstanding the Constitutions of Archbishop Peckham in 1279,[7] headed

> Eucharistia in tabernaculo clauso, idque in pixide decenti, ne alteratur, custodiatur, et singulis Dominicis innovetur.

The distinction between the tabernacle and the pyx is specified by Lyndwood, the great English canonist, who thinks it necessary to say in his Gloss, " Sic ergo tabernaculum et pyxis non supponunt pro eodem, quia pyxis poni debet in tabernaculo, sicut hic patet;" and " Tabernaculum—Sic dictum, quia de tabulis sit factum, vel quia tabulis vel lignis sit impensum."[8]

---

[1] Testamenta Vetusta, p. 154.
[2] Ibid., p. 768.
[3] Ibid., p. 255. It is possible that these last examples might have been chiefly intended for use in the Easter sepulchre ceremonies.
[4] Nichols; Illustrations, &c., pp. 93 and 102.
[5] Inventory of Goods of Westminster Abbey ; London and Middlesex Archæological Transactions, IV, p. 319.
[6] Rock ; Church of our Fathers, IV, p. 208.
[7] Johnson ; Canons.
[8] Lyndwood, tit. 247; edition of 1679, p. 248. His work must have been compiled before the middle of the fifteenth century, as he died in 1446.

Abroad, especially in Germany (where it is called the
"Sacrament-Hauslein"), many earlier tabernacles may be
seen, dating back some fifty years previously. It will suffice
to refer to the magnificent specimen of Adam Kraft's work at
Nuremburg, which is a canopy of open pinnacles and tracery
64 feet high; and to Ulm, Ratisbon, Paderborn, Limburg,
and Meissen.[1] The grandest of all is at Seville Cathedral,
called *El Monumento*; it was designed by Antonio Florentin
in 1544, and added to in 1624 and 1688; composed of twenty-
four columns in each stage, and rising to a height dispro-
portionate even to the cathedral itself which is 145 feet to the
vaulting. This, however, is not a permanent structure, but
takes to pieces and is only put up for the festival of Corpus
Christi and the ceremony of the Easter sepulchre.[2]

THE CRUETS.

The cruets to supply the chalice may be briefly noticed.

The Excerptions of Ecbright, A.D. 740,[3] say as follows:
"Let the priests of God always diligently take care that the
bread and wine and water (without which masses cannot be
celebrated) be pure and clean; for if they do otherwise they
shall be punished with them who offered to our Lord vinegar
mixed with gall, unless penitence relieve them."[4]

The *Capitula* of Theodulph, in 994, direct that both the
oblation, and the wine and the water that belong to the offering of the mass-song, be provided, and regarded with all
purity and diligence and with fear of God, and that nothing
be done unchastely or impurely; for there can be no mass-
song without these three things; viz., the oblation, the wine,

---

[1] Examples are engraved by Lubke, pp. 223 and 225.
[2] Descripcion del Templo Catedral de Sevilla, pp. 153 and 193.
[3] Johnson; Canons. These Excerptions are always so called, but
modern examination shows that they are not of this date, though early.
[4] Johnson; Canons. We need not be very much surprised that the
lay judges of the Privy Council were ignorant of the requirements of
canon law; but the fact only renders more apparent the folly of setting
technical questions, relating to an entirely special and peculiar branch of
law, to be decided by those who not only have never attempted to make
ecclesiastical law their study, but are even unacquainted with its simplest
terminology.

and the water. As the Holy Writ says : Let the fear of God be with you, and do all that is here with great carefulness.[1]

In the Canons of 960 it is ordered that a priest never presume to celebrate mass unless he hath all things appertaining to the housel; viz., a pure oblation, pure wine and pure water. Wóe be to him that begins to celebrate unless he have all these.[2]

The cruets needed to supply the chalice with wine and water, having an honourable office though of secondary importance, were more or less costly; thus, for example, the Earl of Warwick, in 1400, bequeathed to the Chapel of Our Lady of Warwick, with his best censer and a chalice, two cruets of silver gilt made in the shape of two angels.[3] Sir William Depeden, in 1402, leaves to certain chantries two silver cruets;[4] and Beatrice, Lady de Roos, in 1414, bequeathed to the high altar of the Priory of Wartre, amongst other silver things, " ij phialas." [5]

After the celebration it was directed that the sacred vessels should be carefully cleansed. The Constitutions of Archbishop Edmund, in 1236, give the following directions:—At the celebration of the mass let not the priest, when he is going to give himself the Host, first kiss It, because he ought not to touch It with his mouth before he receives It. But if, as some do,[6] he takes It off from the paten, let him after mass cause both the chalice and paten to be rinsed in water, or else only the chalice, if he did not take It from the paten. Let the priest have near to the altar a very clean cloth, cleanly and decently covered, and every way inclosed, to wipe his fingers and lips after receiving the Sacrament of the Altar.[7]

The recess in the wall on the south of the altar, called the piscina, is intended to receive and carry away the rinsings;

---

[1] Johnson ; Canons.
[2] Johnson ; Canons. See *ante*, p. 62, note [4].
[3] Testamenta Vetusta, p. 154.
[4] Testamenta Eboracensia, I ; Surtees Society, p. 295.
[5] Ibid., p. 378.
[6] Lyndwood's Gloss says : that is, without taking it up in his fingers, and so putting the paten to his mouth, as most of the Religious (the monastic Orders) do.
[7] Johnson ; Canons.

it has a shallow basin in the cill, with a drain, and in the fourteenth century there were often two such basins and drains,
one being presumably for the rinsings of the chalice, and one
for those of the celebrant's hands. The drain is carried in
the substance of the wall into the ground beneath. Very
usually the piscina had a shelf across it, half way up, which is
supposed to have served as a credence, but its extreme nar-
rowness militates against the presumption; the still existing
shelf is frequently of wood, though of very early, and probably original date. In Northern Europe an altar invariably
had its piscina, and where one exists it offers sure evidence
that an altar once existed closely in proximity; but in
Southern Europe such a thing very rarely occurs; I do not
recollect one. On the other hand, the credence, unless the
shelf just mentioned served as such, was a thing absolutely
unknown here, both in name and in fact.[1] A stone table at
St. Cross, Winchester, is sometimes referred to as an English
example; but probably the structure was monumental: and
the word is simply the Italian "*credenza*" anglicised.

The MANILIA was a metal vessel from which water for the
lavation of the hands was poured through a long spout, and
was usually made in some fantastic form, as of an animal or
siren.[2] Probably its possession was limited to the larger and
wealthier of the cathedrals and monasteries.

THE CROSS.

We now come to the cross. We learn that when the
Emperor Constantine and the Empress St. Helena deposited
the body of St. Peter in the Basilica, they placed over the
shrine a cross of pure gold weighing 150 lbs.;[3] but we cannot
be sure that this was in connection with the altar. Riddle

---

[1] Notwithstanding which, a credence was decided to be a legal ornament
of the church, while an altar of stone was forbidden by the Arches Court
(overruling the diocesan court), in the St. Sepulchre, Cambridge, Case.
(*Faulkner* v. *Litchfield and Stearn*, reported 1 Robertson, 184, and 3 Notes
of Cases, 510.)

[2] An example is engraved in Lubke's work, p. 153.

[3] Parker; Archæology of Rome, XI, p. 64.

states that crosses do not appear to have been set up in churches until about the middle of the fourth century.[1] Haydn says the cross was brought into use for devotional purposes in churches and chambers about the year 431.[2] In fact it would appear that, until about the tenth century, it was not customary to leave any ornament standing on the altar except during the time of mass, but at that period a cross was usually kept there as part of its ordinary furniture.[3] In a manuscript of the ninth century, upon the altar covered with a table-cloth, there are represented a chalice, wafer, and cross.[4] According to Dr. Rock, it always stood there in the Anglo-Saxon period.[5] Subsequently it at all times formed part of the furniture of the altar; generally, though not invariably, flanked by candlesticks.[6] In the Eastern Church it always stands on the altar between two candlesticks.

Gifts and bequests of crosses were very common, and one example will suffice. The Duke of Bedford, Regent of France, bequeathed, in 1434, to the church in which he might be buried, "unam crucem argenteam deauratam, cum buretis, quas habuit de redemptione Johannis Alcurons."[7]

At what time the figure was added to the cross (making it a crucifix) does not appear with any certainty. Haydn's Dictionary says that it was first used in the fourth century, and came into general use in the eighth century.[8] In the earlier representations of the crucifixion, our Lord's feet are invariably shown as affixed to the cross by separate nails, up to (roughly) the fourteenth century, and the change to the figure with one nail passing through both feet was not invariable for long afterwards. The single nail is clearly opposed to tradition;

---

[1] Riddle ; Christian Antiquities, p. 706.
[2] Haydn ; Dictionary of Dates, *s. v.*
[3] Walcott ; Sacred Archæology, *s. v.* "*Altar.*"
[4] Lacroix ; Military and Religious Life, engraving at p. 277.
[5] Rock ; Church of our Fathers, I, p. 269.
[6] In illustrations to an edition of the Legenda Aurea, printed at Lyons in 1519, the cross alone is seen standing on the altar (ffs. clxix and clxxxij).
[7] Nichols ; Royal Wills, p. 272.
[8] Haydn ; Dictionary of Dates, *s. v.*

F

and the removal of the hypopodion, and the substitution at the same time of one nail for two, was a change which has been attributed by some authorities to the Albigensian schismatics.[1]

Upon crosses of all kinds, and especially those for the altar, wealth of art and material were lavished in token of honour. Gold and silver-gilt were common up to the end of the twelfth century, and the whole was most usually covered with rich enamel ; afterwards chiefly metal gilt and enriched with gems. At an early date[2] arose the saying, subsequently put into English rhyme :—

> In the good old times, the times of old,
> The cross was of wood and the bishop of gold ;
> Now times have changed, and are not so good,
> The cross is of gold and the bishop of wood.[3]

Amongst the goods of the Chapel of St. Stephen, Westminster, was a cross of gold, set with stone and pearl, and weighing 27 oz.[4]

It is well known that Queen Elizabeth had a cross and candlesticks upon the altar of her private chapel, and it need scarcely be said that they were in use in the church revival under the auspices of Archbishop Laud. It is related, for example, that the saintly Nicholas Ferrar, in 1625, had one in his church at Little Gidding.[5]

THE CANDLESTICKS.

At a very early date, we hear of lamps presented to churches, and must presume, from the fact of their being formed of precious metals and rich workmanship, that they were by no means intended for the mere purpose of giving necessary light to the building ; in fact, the extract from

---

[1] Walcott ; s. v. "*Cross.*"
[2] It appears in the Works of St. Boniface. (Walcott.)
[3] I need scarcely say that the quotation is not given in reference to our own diocesan, for whom every one must entertain a very sincere respect.
[4] London and Middlesex Archæological Transactions, IV, p. 371.
[5] Hierurgia Anglicana, p. 28.

Myrc's Instruction to the Parish Priest, in the middle of the fifteenth century (see p. 69, *post*), shows clearly enough the importance of the light in a liturgical point of view.

The origin of the practice, like that of so many other adjuncts to divine worship, is probably derived from the use in the Temple, of which we read that Bezaleel (B.C. 1491) made "a candlestick of pure gold" for the Tabernacle.[1]

Amongst the costly gifts of the Emperor Constantine and the Empress St. Helena, to the Basilica of St. Peter, Rome, in the year 320, were a candelabrum 10 feet high, with 4 imitation gold candlesticks with silver incrustations representing the Acts of the Apostles, and a gold corona, being a beacon with 50 dolphins serving as lamps, and weighing 35 lbs. ; 32 silver lamps in the choir, with dolphins (*i. e., en suite*), each 10 lbs., and at the right of the altar 30 silver lamps, each 8 lbs.[2] And so Pope Hilary (pope from 461 to 467), gave to St. Peter's 24 silver candlesticks, each weighing 5 lbs.[3]

In the middle of the ninth century, Pope Leo. IV (pope from 845 to 857), when rebuilding the Church of SS. Quattro Coronati, Rome, gave a gold corona to hang over the high altar, with a gold cross in the midst, having fourteen jewels, of which five were fixed in the cross and the other nine hanging from it; and afterwards a corona of silver weighing 25 lbs.; to the Oratory of St. Barbara he gave a silver corona weighing 12 lbs., and 10 silver lamps.[4]

At the Church of San Clemente, Rome, in a mosaic picture made between 1049 and 1055, lamps are seen hanging from arches, in addition to the candlesticks on the altar.[5] Of not much later date is a very beautiful corona, still preserved in the church at Hildesheim,[6] a singularly quaint and unaltered

---

[1] Exodus xxv, 31.
[2] Parker; Archæology of Rome, XI, p. 64.
[3] Ibid., p. 65.
[4] Ibid., p. 61.
[5] Ibid., p. 58.
[6] Engraved in Caumont's Abécédaire (Religieuse), p. 293; also in Lubke, p. 173.

little town some thirty miles south of Hanover.   It is, however, necessary to limit my remarks to the altar-candlesticks.

Lyndwood refers to the writings of St. Isidore of Seville, in the seventh century, wherein he states that under the type of this corporeal light, that Light is shown forth of which we read in the Gospel, " He was the true Light which lightened every man;" so burning it signifies Christ himself, the Brightness of Eternal Life.   The Canons of 960 direct that a light be always burning in church when mass is sung.[1]

But Lubke, a very eminent and careful authority in such matters, says that they can be proved not to have stood on the altars before the twelfth century.[2]   (The mosaic I have just referred to is, however, half a century earlier.)   Caumont gives the representation of an enamelled example dating in this century.[3]   Walcott says that, before the thirteenth century, no candles or crosses were permitted to be permanently set on altars, but they were invariably brought in by two acolytes when mass was to be said.[4]

By the Canons of 1322, under Archbishop Walter Reynolds, it is ordered [5] :—

> Nullus clericus permittatur ministrare in officio altaris nisi indutus sit superpellicio, et tempore quo Missarum Solemnia peraguntur accendantur duæ candelæ, vel ad minus una.

Amongst innumerable examples two or three will suffice, the first of which will show the importance attached to the light.

In Myrc's Instruction for the Parish Priest (c. 1450), he says :—

> Al oþer thynge þow knowest wel
> What þe nedeth every del
> Loke þat þy candel of wax hyt be,
> And set hyre, so þat þow hyre se,

---

[1] Johnson; Canons.
[2] Lubke; Ecclesiastical Art in Germany, English ed., p. 175.
[3] Caumont; Abécédaire, p. 290.
[4] Walcott; Sacred Archæology, *s. v.* "*Altar.*"   Here again we must regret his system of omitting, for the sake of brevity, references to his authorities; we can, therefore, form no opinion whether the statement is trustworthy, or the reverse.
[5] Gibson; Codex, p. 471.

On þe lyfte half of þyn autere.
And loke algate ho brenne clere :
Wayte þat ho brenne in alle wyse
Tyl þou have do þat servyse.[1]

And zef þow be so unwys
þat þow synge by malys,
Withowte water and ly3t also,
And wost welle þe wonteth bo,
þow schalt þenne for þy songe
Bope wepe and weyle er a-monge,
Tyl þe byschope of hys ore
To þy sonse the restore.[2]

The Church of St. Mary-at-Hill possessed, in the year
1485-6 (as appears by an inventory of the church goods), on
the high altar two great candlesticks and three small ; and on
St. Stephen's altar two more.[3] In a work printed at Lyons
in the same year, in a woodcut of St. Lupus communicating
King Clothair there appear upon the altar only the chalice
and two small candles ; the rood, with SS. Mary and John, is
on the reredos behind.[4]

In the Manuale Curatorum, published at Basle in 1514, we
find, amongst the *Articuli contra clerum,* " In aliquis, &c., aut
sine lumine celebraverit." [5]

As an illustration of the value of silver candlesticks we
may cite the case of St. Mary-at-Hill, where were—[6]

A payer of candellsteks off selver parcell gylt, off
  ye gyfte of Mast^r Hugh Pemberton some time
  alderman of London . . . . . . iij^{xx} xi unc.

and the bequest to Faversham Church, by John Hatch, in
1533, of £20 towards buying a pair; and at Westminster
Abbey, at the dissolution, there were pairs of silver candlesticks weighing respectively 100 oz., 72 oz., 92 oz., and 97 oz.[7]

---

[1] Myrc's Instructions for the Parish Priest ; Early English Text Society,
p. 57.
[2] Ibid., p. 62.   [3] Nichols; Illustrations, &c., p, 115.
[4] Legenda Aurea ; fol. Lyons, 1486: No. CXXIII.
[5] Manuale Curatorum Predicandi prebens modum, Lib. II, conside-
ratio xx, fol. cxviij.
[6] Nichols ; Illustrations, p. 271.
[7] Westminster Inventory ; London and Middlesex Archæological
Transactions, IV, 319.

At South Ockendon, Essex,[1] amongst the

> Thyngs that were sold syth the Kyng's ma^{ties}, that now is, was crowned ;
>
> In p'mis Robet Fenwyck and Humfrey Gyll sold on great payr of candelstyks y^t stode befor ye alt̃, t̃ ij lytle payre of candelstyks that stode upon the alt̃.

King Edward VI ordered that, since images had been abused by pilgrimages, no lights should thenceforth be set before any image or picture, " but onely twoo lightes upon the high aulter, before the Sacrament, which, for the significacion that Christe is the very true light of the worlde, thei shall suffre to remain still." [2]

And so, in Cranmer's Visitation Articles, he enquired whether they suffer any torches, candles, tapers, or other lights to be in your churches, but only two lights upon the high altar.[3]

The use of candles was of course restored in the Laudian revival; as, for instance, Nicholas Ferrar had them in his church at Little Gidding; [4] and in Smart's sermon at Durham Cathedral, on 27th July, 1628, he charged Bishop Cosens, *inter alia*, with having tapers upon the altar.[5]

In recent times, even the Privy Council have held that candlesticks upon the altar-ledge are legal decorations, but they objected to the candles being lighted; which simply reminds one of Cowper's fable of the controversy between eyes and nose, when the spectacles set them at wrong, and the judgment, that whenever the nose put its spectacles on, whether by daylight or candlelight, eyes should be shut.

The number of candles adopted as the rule of the English Church appears to have been, in this and in so many other things, a re-enactment of the custom or practice of the very early Church; and we find it still customary in

---

[1] Essex Archæological Transactions, N. S., II, p. 188.

[2] Injunctions of Edward VI, in 1547. Sparrow ; Collection, 2. And Cardwell ; Documentary Annals, I, p. 7.

[3] Cranmer ; Visitation Articles. Sparrow ; Collection, 26. Cardwell ; Documentary Annals.

[4] Hierurgia Anglicana, p. 28.

[5] Brand ; Popular Antiquities (Bohn's Ed., II, 320).

the unchanging East. And the same use may be seen in
North Italy, as at Venice and Lucca for example, where the
two altar-candlesticks stand on a low step, while the four
candles on the altar are not always lighted; in addition there
is often a branch candlestick on a pivot at the outer end of a
low wall running out at either end of the altar. In Spain,
four candles are common. The most usual modern Roman
practice is to have six large candles, but I doubt if this
number was in any case introduced before the seventeenth
century. Twelve may be found earlier. The minimum of
one at the least, is shown in several of the wood engravings
in the History of the Cross, printed in 1483.[1]

In referring to candlesticks we must not omit to advert to
Judases. Candles being made of vast size and thickness, it
became common to construct the lower part standing upon
the pricket of the candlestick, of wood painted to look like
wax and possibly sometimes coated with it; and upon this the
real candle was set. These false candles were called Judases;
St. Margaret, Westminster, furnishes an example [2]:—

\ 1524. Paid for twelve Judacis to stand with the tapers, ij*.

THE PAX.

The pax is a small tablet, six or eight inches long by a less
width, with a handle like that of a jug or lanthorn at the
back, and very generally formed of metal, which is often
enriched with enamel. The name in early English was pax-
brede,[3] from pax-board, indicating that it was or had been
commonly formed of wood; but the more general name is the
osculatorium, from its object in respect to the osculum pacis,
and less commonly by other names, as asser ad pacem, paxillum, tabula pacis, and deosculatory.[4] Originally, the kiss of
peace was given by the officiating priest to the deacon, by him

---

[1] Xylographic History of the Cross, printed in 1483; fac simile reprint,
edited by Berjeau, 4to, London, 1863; illustrations to vv. 48, 50 and 64.
[2] St. Margaret, Westminster, 1524. (Nichols; Illustrations, p. 9.)
[3] For example; in the Inventory of St. Mary-at-Hill, in 1431-2:
"iij paxbredes of sylver gilt." (Nichols; Illustrations, &c., p. 94.)
[4] Walcott.

to others, and so conveyed to the whole congregation; but when, before long, the inconveniences of the system became apparent, a tablet called the pax was introduced, and the priest gave to it the kiss of peace, and it was passed on to the rest.

According to authorities cited by Canon Simmons, the use of the pax began in the thirteenth century, but he believes it to have been rather earlier.[1] Haydn's Dictionary of Dates says, about the twelfth century.[2] It was one of the articles which, under Archbishop Gray's Constitutions, in 1250, were to be provided by the parishioners for the use of the church.[3]

In illustration of the use in England, we may refer to the Constitutions of Archbishop Edmund Rich, in 1236, which directed that priests' concubines be monished by the archdeacons, &c., either to marry, enter a cloister, or do public penance, in default of which they were to be denied the pax, &c.[4] Representations of the pax standing upon the altar frequently appear in early paintings, illuminations, and sculpture, and in the woodcuts to early-printed books. The church at St. Mary-at-Hill had, in 1431, three paxbredes of silver gilt.[5] One at Florence, which was ornamented with the engraving called Niello, is memorable as being the first engraved plate from which a printed impression was taken. The pax was wrought by Maso Finiguerra in 1452 for the baptistery of San Giovanni, Florence, and the print from it exists in the National Library at Paris.[6] A pax, preserved in the treasury at Arezzo, was given in 1464 by Pope Pius II to his fellow citizens of Sienna, who afterwards presented it to Arezzo.[7]

I believe that the Book of the Gospels was not infrequently used instead of a separate article. Such was the case at

---

[1] Lay Folks' Mass Book; Early English Text Society, p. 296.
[2] Haydn's Dictionary of Dates, s. v.
[3] Johnson; Canons.
[4] Ibid. The ordinance seems to have been ineffectual, for we find further penalties enacted by the Legatine Constitutions of Othobon in 1268.
[5] Inventory of the Goods of St. Mary-at-Hill.
[6] Labarte, p. 249.
[7] Ibid., p. 251.

Durham Cathedral, where was a marvellous fair Book of the
Epistles and Gospels, on the silver cover of which was a
picture of the Saviour, which book served for a pax.[1]

THE BOOKS.

Various books were needed for the service of the altar.
First, the Missal; next the Sacramentarium, which was nearly
the same; the Evangelarium, or Evangelistarium, containing
the Gospels; the Lectionarium, containing the Epistles; the
Benedictionarium and the Antiphonarium. Thus, at St. Mary-
at-Hill, in 1504, they[2]

> Paid to the bokebynder at Ledon Halle for coveryng,
> bynding, and pesyng 4 antiphonars, a book, a manuell,
> a legend, 2 solomes, and 3 grayles £2 6 8

By the Canons, temp. King Edgar, it was ordered that a
priest should never celebrate mass without book, but that the
Canon (of the Mass) should be before his eyes to see to, if
needed, lest he mistake; and further, that every priest shall
take great care to have a good book, or at least a true
(correct) one.[3] So in Theodulph's *Capitula*, in 994, the Holy
Books are spoken of as amongst the essentials of a church.[4]

Mass-books were, of course, very generally destroyed in
the time of King Edward VI, and King James I forbade
their re-introduction into the country under penalties.[5]

CUSHIONS.

The little book-desks which so usually stand upon altars, and
are practically very convenient (if invented before quite modern
times), were extremely rare, but cushions were customarily
used to rest the book (not the priest's elbows) upon. In the
Salisbury Cathedral Inventory, in the thirteenth century, it

---

[1] Rites of Durham; Surtees Society, p. 7.
[2] Nichols; Illustrations, p. 105.
[3] Johnson; Canons.
[4] Ibid.
[5] Gibson; Codex.

appears they had *Lectricum unum pro altare;* and at another altar, *Pulvinaria ij. quod unum est de serico.*[1] And at Westminster Abbey, in 1388, were *Cervicalia.*[2] In the fifteenth century they are often represented in woodcuts, and very frequently bequeathed by wills to altars and chapels. In fact, they seem to have become quite usual by the time of the Reformation, and are constantly mentioned in the inventories of church goods at that date, under various spellings, such as quissen, quishwine, qwissinge, quusson or cussen, cuyshyne and chosin, and are spoken of later as pillows. At King's Langley, Hertfordshire, for example :—[3]

> A cuyshyne of grene sylke for the hyghe alter ;
> It^m ij old pyllowes for the awlters.

At St. Mary-at-Hill, in 1498, were [4]

> Four gret quysshons with downe, 2 of them with sylke, and 2 with fustean ;

while in their inventory in 1562 [5] appear two cushions of cloth of gold and crimson velvet, two of green velvet with escutcheons of needlework, two cloth of bawdkyn, and a little cushion with a tree of green silk. Amongst the Lincolnshire church goods, temp. Edward VI,[6] was "a pillowe which line (lay) on thaltare, gevin to a maide to make her a stomacher of."

At North Ockenden, Essex, "a chosin of fuchen in napulls, byindard of rede and yowls sarssenit."[7]

FLOWERS.

The authority always quoted in evidence that at an early period it was customary to set flowers upon altars, is the famous work of St. Augustine the Great, *De Civitate Dei.* It narrates that a certain man went to the shrine of St. Stephen,

---

[1] Rock ; Church of our Fathers, IV, p. 108.
[2] London and Middlesex Archæological Transactions, V, p. 428.
[3] Cussans ; Hertfordshire Inventories, p. 52.
[4] Nichols ; Illustrations, &c., p. 76.
[5] Ibid., p. 115.
[6] Peacock ; Lincolnshire Church Goods, p. 120.
[7] A cushion of fustian of Naples, bound with red and yellow sarsenct. (Essex Archæological Transactions, N. S, II., p. 186.)

and prayed earnestly for Martial, his father-in-law, a Pagan, then lying on his death-bed ; and when he departed he took from the altar the first flower that came to hand, and put it, for it was now night, at the head of his father-in-law, who was asleep, and who, by its silent instrumentality, was converted and sought baptism.[1]

From the fact of flowers being thus mentioned in connection with one individual, and but once by him, we can only draw the inference that it was not the general practice to employ them for the decoration of altars. I do not remember to have seen them represented in any very ancient work of art, the oldest I have noted being a painting, dated 1573, by Sebastian Vraux, where vases for flowers are represented ; and where we read of them in parish accounts they are only for strewing or general decoration of the church, or perhaps (as at St. Margaret Pattens, in 1524) for garlands for the choir on Corpus Christi Day and the Festival of the Patron. At all events, it seems quite clear that they were not, at an early date, set upon the altar itself, but on the shelf. The practice of decorating altars with flowers placed upon the shelf can be scarcely said to prevail anywhere except amongst churches of the " High Church " type in England. In France, the sanctuary is very usually decorated with cut flowers and plants in pots, and wreaths of evergreens (frequently artificial) at the commencement, and more or less during the period of the " Month of Mary " (May), but the origin of that festivity is perfectly modern ; while in Italy, with its wealth of flowers, we seldom or never see used for the purpose any but tawdry artificial plants and flowers, fit in every way for ornaments of a second-rate music-hall. If not used for the adornment of the altar, there can be no doubt that the practice of decorating the church with flowers and branches of trees is of great antiquity.[2]

But although there may be but little to be said in an

---

[1] St. Augustine ; De Civitate Dei, Lib. XXII, c. viii. (Church Press Company, 1869, p. 17.)

[2] Riddle ; Manual of Christian Antiquities, p. 706.

archæological point of view for flowers as a decoration for the
altar, they seem to possess an inherent or natural appropriate-
ness, which without pausing to analyze the feeling, is at once
perceptible, while no practical or tangible reason has ever
been urged against them.[1] On the other hand stands the fact
that in no work of the creation is beauty, fitness, and organiza-
tion more fully displayed. Admiration and love of flowers
being inherent in the human breast, it is but a natural instinct
to devote that which we admire and love to the worship of
Him to whom we owe all that we enjoy. The lines of a modern
poet seem singularly appropriate :—

> Bring flowers to the shrine where we kneel in prayer—
> They are nature's offering—their place is there ;
> They speak of hope to the fainting heart ;
> With a voice of promise they come and part.[2]

THE CENSER, THURIBLE, OR SHIP.

The censer or thurible (from *Thus,* frankincense), with its
ship or navicula, as being amongst the items immediately
connected with the service of the altar, must be mentioned,
however briefly.

The origin of the use of the censer in religious worship, of
course dates back to the most remote period in European
history, and probably earlier; and we may fairly conclude
that it descended to Christian worship directly from Jewish
ritualism. The gifts to the infant Saviour were gold, and
frankincense, and myrrh. Its use is seen in sculpture and
painting on very early Christian monuments, and thence
downwards along the course of time. Incense is mentioned in
the so-called Apostolic Canons,[3] which are believed to date
from the earlier part of the fourth century. Lubke states[4]
that, in the mediæval period, the censer resembled the dome of
a building, and was suspended by four chains. I think that

---

[1] There was an interesting correspondence on the subject in the Church
Times of the spring of 1880.
[2] Kenelm Digby ; Compitum ; Road of Nature.
[3] Bingham ; Christian Antiquities, Bk. VIII, c. vi, s. 21, p. 109.
[4] Lubke, p. 151.

an hexagonal form with three chains was more usual. The ship, or navicula, was the vessel which contained incense for the supply of the censer, and was so called from its being very generally made in the form of a ship.

Censers were commonly wrought of rich metal and artistic design and workmanship. Lubke says that, in early times, they were usually made of bronze or copper, and later of silver; but we find that amongst the things presented by Pope Pascal I (A.D. 686) to the Church of St. Cecilia in Trastevere, was a silver gilt thurible weighing 1 lb.[1]

Pope Leo IV, in the middle of the ninth century, presented to the Church of the SS. Quattro Coronati, at Rome, two silver thuribles of 2 lbs. 1 oz. weight. One of about the same date is represented in an illustration to Lacroix' book.[2] At Lille, is one of the twelfth century, of copper gilt, of very elaborate design with fantastic animals in bold relief, and having on the apex an angel and three smaller figures representing Ananias, Azarias and Misael,[3] and in evident allusion to the fiery furnace from the effects of which they were so miraculously preserved.

Theophilus the monk, in his treatise written in the same century, gave directions respecting thuribles.[4] In an inventory of the property of the Duke of Anjou and King Charles V of France, as mentioned by Labarte,[5] are the following examples:—

> Ung grant encencier d'or, pour la chapelle due roy, ouvré à huit chapiteaulx, en facon de maçonnière, et est le pinacle dudi encencier ouvré à huit osteaulx, et est à pié ouvré à jour.
> Ung encencier d'or, à quatre pignons, et à quatre tournelles.

At Westminster Abbey, in 1388, were:[6]—

> Turibuli ij magna, ex dono quondam Regis Henrici III; continentes in summitate ij parvas campanulas.
> Turibulum magnum argenteum deauratum cum ymaginibus in tabernaculis sedentibus; ex dono Dom. Simonis Cardinalis.

Among the bequests of Lady de Roos, in 1414, is "j par

---

[1] Parker; Archæology of Rome, XI, p. 67.
[2] Lacroix; Military and Religious Life in the Middle Ages, p. 277.
[3] Labarte; engraving, p. 221.
[4] Theophilus; Treatise, p. 49. (Labarte, p. 228.)   [5] Labarte, p. 228.
[6] London and Middlesex Archæological Transactions, V, p. 432.

turribulorum argenti."[1]   So William Bruges, Garter-King-at-Arms, in 1449 bequeathed to the Church of St. George within Stamford, " a peyre of censours of sylver, with a ship of sylver for frankincence, and j spone for the same ship, of sylver."   The Duke of Bedford bequeathed " Unum par turribulorum argenteorum ꝇ deauratorum, que noviter fabricari fecit Parisius."[2]   Henry Hatche, in 1533, bequeathed £20 towards buying a pair of silver censers.[3]   So the Earl of Huntingdon, in 1534, bequeathed to the Church of Elyne, near Ashby-de-la-Zouch, a pair of censers of silver and a flat ship of silver-gilt.[4]   Among the goods of the Church at Great Wakering, Essex, there were stolen from the Church in the second year of King Edward VI (1548 or 1549) besides " ij chaleses p'cell gilt, a senser of sylver and a ship of sylver ; " and at Purleygh four years later, " a shipp of sylver."[5]   At Brightlingsea, a chalice, pyx, pax, and ship, together weighing 89 oz., were sold for £20 : 5s. 3d.; and a pyx, bell, and two candlesticks weighing 57½ oz., were sold for £12 : 18s. 9d.[6] At St. Mary-at-Hill, in 1562, were " ij sheppis of sylver."[7] By the Canons of Archbishop Gray, and others subsequently, censers were ordered to be provided by the parishioners for the use of the church.

Though disused and discountenanced by the Puritan side, the censer continued partially in use.   Thus, the furniture of Bishop Andrews' Chapel comprised " A triquertral censer, wherein the clerk putteth frankincense at the reading of the first lesson.   The navicula, like the keel of a boat, with a half cover and foot, out of which the frankincense is poured ;"[8] and Archbishop Sancroft published a form for the consecration of a censer.[9]   The frankincense was either poured from the ship, or a spoon was used.

[1] Testamenta Eboracensia ; Surtees Society, I, p. 378.
[2] Nichols ; Royal Wills, p. 372.
[3] Testamenta Vetusta, p. 662.
[4] Nichols ; Testamenta Vetusta, p. 660.
[5] Inventory of Essex Church Goods ; Essex Archæological Society.
[6] Nichols ; Testamenta Vetusta, p. 14.
[7] Nichols ; Illustrations, p. 93.
[8] Prynne ; Canterbury's Doom, p. 122.
[9] Archbishop Sancroft's Form of Dedication of a Church or Chapel, published in 1685. (See Hierurgia Anglicana, p. 180, et seq.)

The offering annually presented at the festival of the
Epiphany, by or on behalf of the Queen, upon the altar of
the Chapel Royal, of gold and frankincense and myrrh, will
be borne in mind.

THE SACRING, SANCTUS, OR SANCTE-BELL.

This is the last of the ornaments of the church to which I
have to advert in immediate connection with the altar.

At what precise date arose the practice of employing a
bell to give notice of the moment when the highest act of
Christian worship was celebrated, is uncertain, but it appears
to have been customary in the thirteenth century.[1] It would,
of course, be objectless in a small building; but more probably
it was, like the censer, a survival from the worship of the
earlier dispensation. As edifices of grander dimensions were
obtained and filled with worshippers, the practical use of the
bell became obvious. In the manuscript dating in the ninth
century, already adverted to, the bell is represented.[2] The
Lay Folks' Mass Book refers to it thus[3] :—

> þen tyme is to þe sacrynge
> A litel belle men oyse to ryng.
> þen shal þou do reverence
> to ihesu crist awen presence.

Gifts and bequests of such bells made of the precious
metals, are very frequently recorded. Thus, in 1356 Elizabeth,
Countess of Northampton, bequeathed to the Church of the
Friars Preachers, in London, a silver bell.[4] Sir John Depeden,
in 1402, bequeathed "j campanam de argento; videlicet,
j sacring bell;"[5] and Lady de Roos, in "1414, j tintinnabulum
argenti;"[6] William Bruges, Garter-King, in 1449, "a little
hand-bell of Sylver, of the gretnesse of a sacrynge bell;"[7] and
Sir Thomas Lyttleton, Justice of the Common Pleas, in 1481,

---

[1] Canon Simmons; Notes to Lay Folks' Mass Book; Early English
Text Society, p. 272.
[2] Lacroix; engraving, p. 277.
[3] Lay Folks' Mass Book; Early English Text Society, p. 37.
[4] Testamenta Vetusta, p. 268.
[5] Testamenta Eboracensia, I, p. 295; Surtees Society.
[6] Ibid., p. 376.   [7] Lambeth Register, 187; Stafford.

bequeathed a sacring bell of silver.[1] At Monken Hadley,
Middlesex, the saunce bell (evidently external) is spoken of
as being 1 foote iij ynces in wydnes (wideness, diameter).[2]
At South Ockenden, Essex, was " a hand-bell in weight iij li.,
and a sancts bell in weyght xx iiij li." [3]

In some parts of Tyrol, three bells are arranged on a tri-
angular frame, and necessarily rung together; they are often
left carelessly on the altar-step. I have seen, in one instance,
a number of such little bells arranged on a wheel, and set
ringing as the wheel revolves; this arrangement appears to
date from the fifteenth century, but there may be doubt as
to the use, since it is fixed at the west end of the cathedral.
A similar example, at Genoa, is shown in an engraving in
Lubke's work.[4]

The sancte-bell was often outside the church, and was a
moderate-sized bell of ordinary bell-metal, set in a small arch,
ordinarily on the eastern gable of the nave. Many examples
remain in England, but the practice does not seem to have
been usual, although it was ordered by the canons of Archbishop Peckham, in 1281, that bells should be tolled at the
elevation of the Body of Christ, in order that the people who
had not leisure daily to be present at mass might, wherever
they were, in houses or fields, bow their knees, in order to the
obtaining the indulgences granted by many bishops.[5]

The hand-bell was one of the items of church goods which,
in the time of King Edward VI, were sold, if of any value, or
else otherwise disposed of; as at Waddington St. Peter,
Lincolnshire, where the churchwardens reported to the Commissioners[6] that there had been—

> one sacringe bell wᶜʰ honge at a may pole topp, and what is
> become of it we know not.

---

[1] Testamenta Vetusta, p. 364.

[2] History of Monken Hadley, by the Rev. Frederick C. Cass ; London
and Middlesex Archæological Transactions, IV, p. 282.

[3] Essex Archæological Transactions, N. S., II, p. 187.

[4] Lubke ; Ecclesiastical Art, p. 154.

[5] Johnson ; Canons. Lyndwood's Glossary, upon *Bells* in the plural,
says it relates to churches in the plural, and that one bell to each church
suffices. (Lyndwood's Provinciale, p. 231.)

[6] Peacock ; Lincolnshire Church Furniture, p. 157.

It was forbidden, by the Royal Injunctions in 1549, and Ridley's Visitation Articles in 1550,[1] but was revived in the following reign; as at St. Michael, Cornhill, the church-wardens in 1556,[2]—

> Paide to a carpenter for mendinge the saintes bell, for boltes and iron of the same . . . . ijᵉ

The wholesale destruction of church goods of all kinds, in the middle of the sixteenth century, seems to have been, so far as parish churches were concerned, limited to the short reign of King Edward VI. First, was a Royal Commission in his second year, which appears to have made a tolerably clean sweep of such things, if they were of saleable value; and what became of the proceeds realized has never yet been shown. The king had not even the immoral excuse that his royal father had, viz., that lavish and extraordinary expenditure must be met with a revenue far beyond that which could legally be obtained, and which led him to act in accordance with the precept attributed to Lord Chesterfield, as written for his son's edification: "Get money; honestly, if you can: but get money." We can only suppose (and it is also the most charitable supposition) that the royal youth was simply the tool of those around him; reminding one of the fable of the monkey, the cat, and the chestnuts—they got the chest-nuts, and he the eternal disgrace of wholesale sacrilege. So greedy and grasping was the spirit shown, that a second commission was appointed in the king's sixth and seventh years, and went through the country scraping the cheese-rinds their predecessors had left; but it seems possible that they were in many instances forestalled, for the churchwardens often deposed before them that various things had been plun-dered, but by whom they knew not; and this so frequently happened that I think we may reasonably suppose it to have been done, in many cases, not without the tacit sanction of the wardens, and for the sake of preservation.

---

[1] Cardwell; Documentary Annals, I, pp. 64 and 81.
[2] St. Michael, Cornhill; Churchwardens' Accounts, p. 129.

G

GENERAL INDEX.

Altar: the term and synonymes, 1; use in England, 2; structure and material, 3; form, 5; hollowed for relics, &c., 7;
sarcophagi and baths serving as altars, 7; size, 8; slabs, 8;
several parts, 9; carved front, 9; number of altars, 11; double
facing, 13; position, 14.

Altar Ceremonies: washing, 24; special solemnities, 24; curious
customs connected with it, 24.

Altar Consecration, 17; desecration, canonically, 21; under
Edward VI, 22; subsequent re-erection, 23; destruction
by Puritans, 23; introduction forbidden in A.D. 1605., 23.

Altar, High: definition, 13; position, 13; not to be moved, 14;
position under Puritans, 23.

Altar Ornaments: at first none, 41; when cross permanently, 41;
cross and candlesticks, 41; same in the East, 65, 70.

Altar of St. Peter at St. John Lateran, Rome, 3.

Altars, Minor: number, 10; positions, 14; names, 15; Holy Cross,
14; Jesus altar, 15; Mattin altar, 15.

Altars, Portable: what, 19; synonymes, 19; early use, 19; form
and material, 19; requiring Papal licence, 20.

Altar, Super: see *Super-altar.*

Altare portatile: see *Portable Altars.*

Altare viaticum: see *Portable Altars.*

Altaria jitineraria: see *Portable Altars.*

Asser ad pacem: name for pax, 71.

Baldacchino: what, 34.

Bankers: cushions, 74.

Baths, Ancient: serving as altars, 7.

Bells: see *Sancte-bell.*

Beryll: what, 60, *n.*; used for monstrances, 60.

Books : ordered by early Canons, 73 ; names, 73 ; provided by parish, 73 ; popish, forbidden, 73 ; desk, modern, 73 ; on altar, 74.

Burse : what, 52.

Candlesticks and Candles : derived from Jewish Temple, 67 ; of gold given by Bezaleel, 67 ; gold and silver given by Constantine, 67 ; not permanently placed at first, 68 ; ordered by Canons, 68 ; meaning, 68, 70 ; other mention, 69 ; ordered by Edward VI, 70 ; use by Queen Elizabeth, 66, and in Laudian period, 70 ; in Eastern Church, 65, 70 ; permitted by Privy Council, if unlighted, 70 ; number of candlesticks, 70.

Canons, &c.: A.D. 509, Epone, 4, 17 ; 696, Wihgtred, 24 ; 740, Ecgbriht, 17, 21, n., 62 ; 785, Caelchythe, 46 ; 950, Northumbria, 46 ; 957, Ælfric, 45 ; 960, Edgar, 46, 63, 68 ; 994, Theodulph, 17, 19, 43, 52, 62 ; 1071, Winchester, 45 ; 1075, Canterbury, 4 ; 1138, Legatine, 56 ; 1175, Rheims, 46 ; 1175, Canterbury, 46 ; 1195, Legatine, 46 ; 1200, Canterbury, 56 ; 1222, Canterbury, 46 ; 1227, Gregory IX, 21, n. ; 1229, Winchester, 17 ; 1236, Canterbury, 56, 63, 72 ; 1250, York, 33, 43, 52, 56, 68, 72 ; 1279, Canterbury, 61 ; 1281, Canterbury, 33, 43, 56 ; 1305, Canterbury, 33, 43 ; 1311, Vienne, 59, n.; 1322, Canterbury, 56, 68 ; 1452, Cologne, 60 ; 1590, Toulouse, 7.

Canopy over Altar, 34 ; bells, 39.

Censer : Jewish origin, 76 ; Christian use, 76 ; provided by parish, 70 ; form, 76 ; materials and richness, 77 ; gifts, 77 ; Laudian use, 78 ; Sancroft's form of consecration, 78.

Chalice and Paten : gifts by Constantine, 43 ; gold and silver, 43 ; glass or crystal, 44 ; reverent treatment, 45 ; tin, 45 ; wax, 45 ; wood, 45, 46 ; semi-precious stones and marble, 46 ; horn, 46 ; ivory, 46 ; bequests, 46 ; provided by parish, 46 ; benediction, 48 ; general form, 49 ; two handles, 49 ; component parts, 50 ; burial with priest, 53 ; plunder by Edwardian Commissioners, 47.

Chrism : used at consecration of altar, 17.

Christ's Board : synonyme for altar, 2.

Ciborium : canopy over altar, 34.

Commissioners of Edward VI for Church Goods, 22, 47.

Confessionary : a crypt beneath the choir, 16.

Consecration of Altar, 17 ; chrism used, 17 ; of chalice, 48 ; of censer, 78.

Corona: of gold, gifts by Constantine and others, 67.

Corporal: what, 51.

Corporas or Corporax: what, 54.

Corpus Christi: institution of festival, 59, *n.*

Costers: curtains, 37.

Credence: in England only a shelf of piscina, 74.

Cross: gold, gift of Constantine, 64; when used in worship, 64; in England, 65; in East, 65; permanently on altar, 65; figure added, 65; gifts, 65.

Crucifix: material, 64; gifts, 64, 65; introduction, 65; four nails, 65; three nails, perhaps of schismatic origin, 66.

Cruets: needed under Canons, 62; use, 63; gifts, 63.

Curtains: at ends of altars, 17, 39; dossell, 37.

Cushion: for book, 73.

Cussen: see *Cushion.*

Deosculatory: name for *Pax.*

Desecration of Altar: canonically, 21; under Edward VI, 21.

Destruction of Altars and Furniture in Sixteenth and Seventeenth Centuries, 21, 23, 47.

Dossell Curtains: what, 37.

Easter Sepulchres: altar hollowed for purpose, 7.

Eastern Church: customs, 10, 65, 70.

Ewer: for pyx or monstrance, 60.

Flowers: mention by St. Augustine, 74; shown in painting, 1573, 75.

Frankincense: contained in ship, 76; presentation by Queen, 79.

Frontal: with covering for altar, 27; moveable, 28; names for, 28; material, 29; inappropriate designs, 32; provided by parish, 33.

Gestatorium: name for *Portable Altar.*

God's Board: synonyme for *Altar.*

Holy Table: synonyme for *Altar.*

Ivory: chalices, 46; pyx, 54.

Jacob's Pillar: probable origin of chrism, 17.

Jesus Altar: at Durham, 15.

Lamps: silver, 66.

Lapis portatilis: see *Portable Altar.*

Lectricum : what, 74.
Ledge, Altar : what, 34.
Levels of English Churches and Chancels, 17.
Licence for Portable Altar, 20.
Lights : two enjoined by Edward VI, 70 ; and see *Candlesticks*, 66, &c.

Manilia : form and use, 64.
Marble : chalices made of, 46.
Mensa : the top slab of altar, 8 ; size, 7, 8.
Mensa Domini : synonyme for *Altar*, 1.
Monstrance : use and form, 59 ; gifts, 60.
Monumento, El : tabernacle at Seville, 62.
Munificence : ancient, 26, 31, 38, 43, 64, 67; modern, 27.

Navicula : for supply of censer, 76.

Osculatorium : name for *Pax*.
Ostensorium : synonyme for *Monstrance*.

Pala d'oro : the reredos, or frontal so called, 36.
Paliotto : name for frontal, 28.
Pall : for altar, 28 ; presented at coronation, 33; for chalice, 52.
Paten: gift by Constantine, 43 ; forming cover for chalice, 49; and see *Chalice*.
Pax : form and use, 71 ; date of introduction, 72 ; provided by parish, 72 ; earliest engraved print from, 72 ; Gospels used for, 73.
Pax-brede : name for *Pax*.
Paxillum : name for *Pax*.
Peter, St.: his altar at Rome, 3.
Pillow : cushion for missal, 4.
Piscina: use, 63; marking locality of altar, 64; shelf as credence, 64.
Pontifical : form for benediction of chalice, 48.
Portable Altar : various names for, 19, 20 ; early origin, history, material, and examples, 19 ; licence for, 20 ; bequest of, 20.
Predella : what, 40.
Pulvinaria : cushions on altar, 74.
Puritan Objection to Altars, 23.
Pyx : form, 54; material, 54; suspended, 54; standing, 55; called a Corporax, 54 ; bequests, 55 ; provision by parish, 56 ; ordered by Canons, 56 ; with bells, 57; stolen, 58 ; introduction forbidden, 59.

Pyx, Standing: as distinguished from suspended, 55.

Quishwine, Quissen, Quusson, Qwissinge: see *Cushion.*

Reed: for administration of Holy Sacrament, 53.
Relics: contained in altar, 7, 17.
Reredos: what, 17; richness, 35; of tabernacle-work, 35; the Pala
    d'oro, 36; containing relics, 36; paintings, 36; curtain, 37.
Rood-loft: altar in, 15.
Rydells: curtains, 38; colours, 39: and see *Curtain.*

Sacring-bell: name for sancte-bell, 80.
Sancte-bell: from Jewish Temple, 79; usual in thirteenth century,
    79; bequests, 79; on exterior of church, 80.
Sanctus-bell: name for *Sancte-bell.*
Sarcophagi, Ancient: used for altars, 7.
Shelf, Altar: standing on altar, 34.
Ship: to hold incense, 76.
Singing-bread: what, 57; box for, 57.
Stones, Semi-precious: chalices made of, 46.
Super-altar: altar-shelf, sometimes so called, 20; what, 39; and see
    Portable Altar.
Super-frontal: what, 33.

Tabernacle: ordered (perhaps) by canon, 61; splendid examples, 62.
Table, Lord's: synonyme for *Altar*, 1.
Tabula: name for *Frontal.*
Tabula pacis: name for *Pax.*
Thurible: name for *Censer.*
Triforium: altars in, 15.
Triptych Reredosses, 36.

Vail, or Veil: for altar, 38; for chalice, 52.
Vessels, Sacred: sold by St. Ambrose, 29.
Volto Santo, Lucca: silver frontal to altar, 31.

INDEX OF NAMES.

Ælfric: mention of Christ's board, 3.

Alcurons, John: prisoner of Duke of Bedford, 65.

Almyngham, John: bequest for canopy, 35.

Ambrose, St.: selling church goods, 29.

Ananias, Azarias, and Misael: represented on censer, 77.

Andrews, Bishop: censer in chapel, 78.

Angelbertus, Bishop: donor of silver frontal, 29.

Athanasius, St.: mention of wooden altars, 4.

Augustine the Great, St.: mention of wooden altars, 4; flowers on altar, 74.

Augustine of Canterbury, St.: gift of portable altar, 19.

Aventius, Bishop: consecrating altars, 11.

Bardolph: on theft of pyx, 58.

Baret, John: donor of reredos, 37.

Bedford, Duke of: bequest of cross, 65; of censer, 79.

Beresford-Hope, A. J. B.: munificence, 27.

Bezaleel: gold candlestick, 67.

Bohun, Humphrey de: see *Essex, Earl of*.

Boston, Rev. Sir William: bequest of curtains, 38.

Bruges, William: bequest of pyx, 56; of censer, 78; of bell, 79.

Burton, Richard: mixed chalice in A.D. 1640., 57, *n.*

Charlemagne, Emperor: crusade, 19.

Charles V of France: fine censer, 77.

Comyn, Archbishop: prohibited wooden altars, 5.

Constantine, Emperor: erected altars, 10; valuable gifts, 26, 28, 43, 64, 67.

Cosens, Bishop: candlesticks on altar, 70.

Cranmer, Archbishop: Visitation Articles, 70.

Cuthbert, St.: his supposed coffin and altar, 19.
Cyprian, St.: reference to altar, 10.

Dalby, Archdeacon: reference to curtains, 38.
Day, Bishop: favoured stone altars, 21.
Denis, St.: having portable altar, 19.
Depeden, Sir William: bequest of cruets, 63; bell, 79.
Despencer, Lord: bequest of monstrance, 60.

Edward VI, King: commissioners for church goods, 22, 47.
Elizabeth, Queen: Injunctions respecting altars, 21 ; gold cross in chapel, 66.
England, Queen of: presents frankincense, &c., at altar, 79.
Erasmus: reference to wooden altar, 5.
Essex, Earl of: bequest of chalice, 47.
Eusebius of Cæsarea: reference to altar, 10.
Exeter, Duke of: bequest of gold chalice, 46; of monstrance, 61.

Felix I, Pope: consecration of altar, 17.
Ferrar, Nicholas: cross and candlesticks, 66, 70.
Finiguerra, Maso: engraver of pax, 72.
Florentin, Antonio: artist of Seville tabernacle, 62.

Gibbs, Henry H.: munificence, 27.
Goslin, St.: early chalice, 49.
Gregory the Great, St.: gift of portable altar, 19; Mass of, 42.
Gregory of Tours, St.: altars at Bordeaux, 11.
Gregory IV, Pope: gift of veils, 38.
Guinness, Mr.: munificence, 27.

Harold, King: oath on altar, 7, 24.
Hastings, Lady Katherine: bequest of altars, &c., 20.
Hatche, John: bequest of candlesticks, 70; of censer, 78.
Helena, Empress St.: valuable gifts, 26, 43, 64, 67; and see *Constantine*.
Henry, Emperor: donor of Basle frontal, 30.
Hereford, Earl of: bequest of chalices, 47.
Hexham Priory: altars in triforium, 15.
Hilary, Pope: gift of chalices, &c., 44, 67.
Huntingdon, Earl of: bequest of censers, 78.

Ignatius, St.: reference to altar, 10.

Innocent III, Pope: consecration of altars and churches, 9.
Innocent IV, Pope: licence for portable altar, 20.
Irenæus, St.: reference to altar, 10.

Jewel, Bishop: reference to early Italian customs, 12.
Kempe, Archbishop: licence for portable altar, 20.

Kraft, Adam: artist of tabernacle, 62.
Laud, Archbishop: revival of cross and candlesticks, 66.
Leo the Great, Pope: mention of altars, 11.
Leo IV, Pope: donor of curtains, &c., 38, 67, 77.
Lincoln, Countess of: receiving licence for portable altar, 20.
Lyttleton, Sir Thomas: bequest of bell, 80.

Malmesbury, William of: historian, 4.
Maximinianus, St.: consecrated altar in A.D. 547., 5n.; 27.
Michael, Emperor: gift of curtains, 34, 38; of chalice and paten, 44.
Mullooly, Father: paintings at San Clemente, Rome, 42.

Neville Family: offering stag at altar, 25.
Nicholas IV, Pope: granting licence for portable altar, 20.
Northampton, Countess: bequest of bell, 79.

Optatus: mention of wooden altar, 4.
Osborne, John: bequest of pyx, 55.

Palladius, Bishop: erecting early altars, 12.
Paschal I, Pope: rich gifts, 44, 77.
Paul, St.: mention of altar, 1.
Peter, St.: his altar subsisting at Rome, 3.
Puteo, Borginus de: artist of Monza frontal, 30.

Raventhorp, Sir John: chaplain of Aldwerk, 5.
Reresby, Mr. John: hallowing a chalice, 48.
Ridley, Bishop: Injunctions for destroying altars, 21.
Robinson, John: gift of frontal, 32.
Roos, Lady de: bequest of cruets, 63; censer, 78; bell, 79.
Russell, Richard: bequest of altar, 7.

Sancroft, Archbishop: form of consecration of church, 78.
Smart, Peter: sermon against Bishop Cosens, 70.
Stephen VI, Pope: gift of veils, 38.

Tertullian: reference to altar, 10.
Theodoric, Emperor: built church at Ravenna, 6, *n.*
Theophilus the Monk: on ecclesiastical art, 77.

Vigilius, Pope: refuge at altar, 6.
Vraux, Sebastian: painting by, 75.

Warwick, Earl of: bequest of monstrance, 60; censer, chalice, &c., 63.
Waterlow, A. J.: Accounts of St. Michael, Cornhill, 11, *n.*
Wolsinus: artist of silver frontal, 29.
Worcester Cathedral: Mattin altar, 14; altar restored, 23.
Wulstan, St.: introduction of stone altars, 5.
Wykeham, Bishop: best gold chalice, 46; bequest of monstrance, 61.

York, Duchess of: bequest of frontal, 32.

Zouche, Lady Margaret la: bequest of pyx, 56.

INDEX OF PLACES.

Alban's Abbey, St.: altar against rood-screen, 15.
Alcobaça Cathedral: magnificent reredos, 36.
Alexandria: famous for embroidery, 38.
Alfold Church: silver curtain-rings, 39.
Angers Cathedral: altar bare of ornament, 41.
Angoulême Cathedral: altar under central dome, 14.
Arezzo Cathedral: pax, 72.
Arundel Church: original altar, 8, 22; engraving of, 6; complaint in A.D. 1570., 22.
Assisi Cathedral: altar facing both ways, 13.
Astorga Cathedral: magnificent reredos, 36.
Avignon Cathedral: altars in, 11.

Barnet (Chipping): eleven frontals, 32; cloth for pyx, 55.
Bâsle Cathedral: gold frontal, 29; represented in frontispiece.
Bologna Cathedral: altar facing both ways, 13.
Boppard, on Rhine: altars in triforium, 15.
Bordeaux, St. Peter's: early altars, 11.
Boston Guild: super-altars, 20; embroidered frontal, 32.
Brennes Church: early altars, 11.
Breslau Cathedral: many altars, 11.
Brightlingsea Church: goods lost and sold, 78.
Broughton Castle Chapel: incised crosses on altar, 8.
Buda, Hungary: altars against pillars, 15.
Bury St. Edmund's, St. Mary's: reredos, 37.

Canterbury Cathedral: wooden altar, 5; many altars, 11; basilican use, 12; altar at each end of choir, 13.
Chür Cathedral: splendid reredos, 36.
Como Cathedral: altar of single block, 7.
Compton Church: altar in gallery over chancel, 16.
Constance Cathedral: altar at each end of choir, 13.
Cyprus: famous for embroidery, 38.

Dantzig, St. Mary: many altars, 11.
Deerhurst Church: seats round chancel, 12, 23.
Denge Church: chalice sold, 48.
Dublin, Christ Church Cathedral: munificent restoration, 27.
Durham Cathedral: numerous altars, 11, 32; Chapel of the Nine
    Altars, 15; Jesus altar, 15; early portable altar, 19; altar
    replaced in seventeenth century, 23; stag offered at altar, 25;
    reredos triptych, 36; pyx, 54, 55; candlesticks in A.D. 1628., 70;
    pax, 73.

Elyne Church: censer bequeathed to, 78.
Epone: council held at, 4, 17.

Faversham Church: candlesticks given to, 70.
Florence, Baptistery: pax, 72.
        Sta. Maria Novella: embroidered frontal, 32.
Freiburg Cathedral (Breisgau): altar at each end of choir, 13.

Gall (St.) Cathedral: early building plan, 11.
Genoa: bells on wheel, 80.
Germer, St.: arcaded altar, engraving of, 9.
Gidding (Little): cross and candles in A.D. 1625., 66, 70.
Gloucester Cathedral: altar in triforium, 16.
Gourdon Church: very early chalice, 49.
Guimaraes Cathedral: magnificent reredos, 36.

Hadley (Monken): saunce bell, 80.
Hexham Church: altar in triforium, 15.
Hildesheim Cathedral: corona, 67.

Immensee Church: large altar, 8.
Ireland: wooden altars prohibited, 5.

Jerusalem: Church of Holy Sepulchre, 10.
        Church of St. Mary, Valley of Jehoshaphat, 11.

Kingston-on-Thames Church: deed delivered on altar, 25.
Kremsmünster: very early chalice, 44, 50.
Kyrklyngton Church: pyx left to, 56.

Langley Chapel: seats round chancel, 13; altar set longwise, 23.
Langley (King's) Church: cushions on altar, 74.

Lawling Church: glass chalice, 48.
Leon Cathedral: magnificent reredos, 36; bull offered at altar, 25.
Lille Cathedral: fine censer, 77.
Limburg Cathedral: desecrated altar-slab, 8, *n.*; tabernacle, 62.
London; All Saints', Margaret Street: munificent donor, 27.
 Friars Preachers: bell bequeathed to, 79.
 St. Dionis Backchurch: purchase of chalice, 51.
 St. Katherine by the Tower: gold chalice, 46; monstrance, 61.
 St. Margaret Pattens: flowers, 75.
 St. Mary-at-Hill: hallowing altars, 18; super-frontal, 40; pyx cover, 55; monstrance, 61; candlesticks, 69; pax, 72; books, 73; cushion, 74; censer, 78.
 St. Mary Colechurch: altar sold, 22.
 St. Michael, Cornhill: various altars, 11; reredos, 37; veil and curtains bought, 39; chalices hallowed, 48; hanging pyx, 55; sancte-bell, 81.
 St. Paul's Cathedral: many chantries, 11; modern arrangement, 14; buck offered at altar, 25.
Lucca Cathedral: silver altar, 31; number of candles, 71.

Madrid: altar under central dome, 14.
Maintz Cathedral: altar at each end, 13; emperor seated on altar, 24.
Malta, St. John's: modern dove pyx, 54.
Mayence: see *Maintz*.
Meissen Cathedral: altar against rood-screen, 15; tabernacle, 62.
Melford (Long): stained glass, 5.
Merton Priory: delivering lease on altar, 25.
Milan, St. Ambrogio: silver frontal, 29.
 St. Lawrence: glass chalice broken, 45.
Monza Cathedral: silver frontal, 30.
Münich: portable altar at, 19.

Nancy: chalice of St. Goslin, 49.
Nuremburg: tabernacle, 62.

Ockendon, South: candlesticks, 70; bells, 80.
   North: cushion, 74.
Offley Church: chalice stolen, 48.
Oporto Cathedral: magnificent reredos, 36.
Oviedo Cathedral: portable altar, 19.
Oxford, Keble College Chapel: munificent gift, 27.

Paderborn Cathedral: portable altars, 19; tabernacle, 62.
Padua Cathedral: altar facing each way, 13.
Paris, Hotel Clugny: Bâsle frontal now at, 29.
Pistoia Cathedral: silver frontal, 30; magnificent reredos, 36.
Purleigh Church: cloth for pyx, 55; ship, 78; censer stolen, 78.

Ratisbon Cathedral: altar-block hollowed, 7; tabernacle, 62.
    Baptistery: altar of several blocks, 9.
Ravenna, St. Apollinare Nuovo: early altar, 5, 6—engraving of, 1.
    St. Vitale: Mosaic, 27, 41; engraving of, 28; chalice, 49.
Rayleigh Church: goods sold, 22.
Reading, St. Lawrence: altar and super-altar hallowed, 40.
Regensburg: see *Ratisbon.*
Rheims, Council: material of chalice, 46.
Rome; Catacombs : glass chalices, 44.
    Sta. Cecilia in Trastevere : chalice given to, 77.
    San Clemente : early mosaic and painting, 42; lamps, 67.
    San Giorgio in Velabro : veil given to, 38.
    St. John Lateran : earliest existing Christian altar, 3; cibo-
        rium, 4; seven altars, 11.
    Sta. Maria Maggiore : veil given to, 38.
    San Marco : veil given to, 38.
    St. Peter's Basilica : pope seated on altar, 24.
        Altar, 8; refuge of Pope Vigilius, 6.
    Quattro Coronati : curtains, &c., given to, 67, 77.

Salerno Cathedral: ivory frontal, 31.
Salisbury Cathedral: portable altar, 19; frontals, 32; pillow on
Sarcophagi and baths : used as altars, 8.   [altar, 74.
Sawbridgeworth Church: pyx, 57.
Seville Cathedral: tabernacle, 62.
Shorne, Kent: engraving of chalice represented on brass, 50.
Söest (Weissenkirche): still mediæval, 33; embroidered frontal, 33;
    curtains, 39.
Spain: name of parts of altar, 10.
Speyer Cathedral: see *Spires.*
Spires Cathedral: single block altar, 6; altar under central dome, 14.
Spoleto Cathedral: altar facing each way, 13.
Stambridge Church: wooden chalice, 48.
Stamford, St. George's: bequest to, 56, 78.
Surbiton Church: receiving lease of land on altar, 25.

Tarascon Cathedral: early chalice, 50.
Tewkesbury Church: monstrance left to, 60.
Tillingham Church: glass chalice, 48.
Tong Church: glass chalice, 48.
Toulouse: Council at, 7.
Tournay Cathedral: low choir level, 16; Jesse-tree frontal, 33.
Trent Cathedral: altar under central dome, 14.

Udine Cathedral: position of altar, 15.
Ulm Cathedral: altar against rood-screen, 15; tabernacle, 62.

Venice Churches: straw and glass frontals, 31 ; number of candles, 71.
    St. Mark: silver frontal, 31; Pala d'oro, 36.
Verdun Church: altar at each end, 13.
Vienna, St. Stephen: altars against pillars, 15.
Vienne Church: single-block altar, 7; altar in rood-loft, 15.

Waddington Church: bell desecrated, 80.
Wakering Church (Great): goods stolen, 78.
Warwick, College of Our Lady: bequest to, 63.
Westminster Abbey: super-altar, 20; salmon presented on altar, 25; frontals, 32; curtains, 39; chalices, 47; monstrance, 60, 61; candlesticks, 70; cushions, 74; censer, 77.
    St. Margaret's: pyx stolen, 59; Judases, 71.
    St. Stephen's: pyx, 58; cross, 66.
Wilten Abbey Church: very early chalice, 50.
Winchester Cathedral: bequest to, 61.
    St. Cross: doubtful credence, 64.
Windsor, St. George's Chapel: portable altar, 19.
Worcester Cathedral: Mattin altar, 14; altars re-erected in sixteenth century, 23.

York Minster: lamb offered at altar, 25.
    Hungate Church: bequest to, 7.
Ypres Cathedral: position of altars, 11; low choir level, 16.

ROWORTH & CO. LIMITED, NEWTON STREET, HIGH HOLBORN, W.C.

www.ingramcontent.com/pod-product-compliance
Lightning Source LLC
Chambersburg PA
CBHW020809020726
47495CB00008B/2652